The Long Hunt

Texas Ranger Dan Kennedy is in Amarillo when he hears that his young nephew, Jamie, has been kidnapped from the Rocking K Ranch owned by Dan's father. When the culprits turn out to be the Morgan gang, Dan vows to hunt them down and bring Jamie safely home.

He heads south with ex-ranger and expert tracker Josh Brennan but the Morgan gang soon become aware of their pursuers, leaving Dan and Josh vulnerable to attack. Can they survive this formidable threat and bring Jamie home alive?

The Long Hunt

Alan Irwin

A Black Horse Western

ROBERT HALE · LONDON

© Alan Irwin 2010
First published in Great Britain 2011

ISBN 978-0-7090-9131-8

Robert Hale Limited
Clerkenwell House
Clerkenwell Green
London EC1R 0HT

www.halebooks.com

Typeset by
Derek Doyle & Associates, Shaw Heath
Printed and bound in Great Britain by
CPI Antony Rowe, Chippenham and Eastbourne

ONE

It was a busy time on the big Rocking K Ranch in the south-west of Texas. The spring round-up was in progress. The rancher, Jacob Kennedy was out on the range with all but his two oldest ranch hands. New calves were being branded. Mature beef was being rounded up to hand over to drovers who would drive it north to Dodge City. From there it would be transported by rail to Eastern cattle markets.

Back at the ranch house was the rancher's wife Martha. With her was their younger son Clint, his wife Rebecca and their seven-year-old son Jamie. Also in the house during their working hours were two Mexican women, Carmen and Maria, who helped out with household chores, including the cooking.

Clint would normally have been working on the roundup, but just before it started he suffered a bad fall while breaking in a horse for use as a cowpony. His leg was broken in two places and he was liable to be laid up for several weeks. Clint was in his early twenties, tall and strong, happy in his work on the ranch. He was devoted to Jamie and his wife Rebecca, a slim attractive woman who had been his childhood sweetheart.

Clint's elder brother Dan, in his late twenties, was big and strong like his brother, but had a more even temperament. He had left the ranch four years earlier, to the disappointment of his father who had hoped that both his sons would stay helping him to run the ranch. Dan had a hankering to explore the country outside the confines of the Rocking K. After taking a look at New Mexico Territory, Colorado and Kansas, he rode into the Texas Panhandle.

While in Amarillo he was offered a job as a Texas Ranger, which he accepted. He proved to be a competent and reliable law officer, highly skilled in the use of his weapons. He was presently in line for promotion. During his time with the Texas Rangers he had paid one short visit to the Rocking K, where his father had become reconciled to Dan's decision not to stay on at the ranch.

On the Rocking K the two hands, Radford and Bailey, who were not engaged on the roundup, were carrying out some repairs to the corral fence, not far from the ranch house. Bailey was the first to notice the group of seven riders heading slowly along the valley towards the ranch house. He stopped work and studied the group intently. Radford then did the same.

'They look like strangers to me,' said Bailey.

'Likely they heard about the roundup and they're looking for work. If that's the case, we'll send them on to see Mr Kennedy and the ramrod out on the range.'

Inside the house Martha Kennedy had also seen the approaching riders through a window. Clint and his wife and son were in a bedroom where Clint was lying on the bed. He had been told by the doctor to stay there for the time being.

The group of horsemen rode up to the main door of the house and stopped. The leader was a thickset man, a little over medium height. He was bearded, with a hard ruthless face. His name was Morgan. He had been a member of the guerrilla force led by William Quantrill which, in 1863, had raided the Kansas town of Lawrence at dawn. Savagely, they shot down every man and boy in sight, then set the town on fire. When the guerrilla force was later disbanded Morgan had embarked on a life of crime.

As Bailey and Radford approached the house, they saw Martha Kennedy come out on to the raised boardwalk outside the door to meet the riders. The two hands now had a closer view of the strangers.

'I don't like the look of them,' said Radford. 'They sure don't look like cowhands to me.'

'You're right,' said Bailey. 'Let's go to the bunkhouse and buckle on our six-guns, just in case there's any trouble.'

They changed direction and headed for the bunkhouse. Observing this, Morgan spoke to two of

7

his men, who waited until the two hands had entered the building, then dismounted and ran after them. Martha Kennedy, about to speak to Morgan, started and stared in that direction as two shots were heard from inside the bunkhouse. Half a minute later, the two men who had followed the hands inside came out and rejoined Morgan and the others.

Fearing the worst, Martha spoke to Morgan, still sitting astride his mount.

'What was that shooting?' asked Martha, small in size but big in courage and determination, who had stood resolutely by her husband's side during the long hard years spent building up the Rocking K into a large and highly profitable operation. 'Who are you men? What do you want?'

As Martha finished speaking, she was joined by Rebecca, who had come down from the bedroom at the back of the house, curious about the muffled sound of shooting outside. Uncertain as to what was happening, she stood by Martha's side, looking apprehensively at the tough-looking strangers.

Morgan drew his six-gun. The others followed suit.

'You two women stay exactly where you are,' said Morgan. 'I'll let you know soon enough why we're here.'

They all dismounted and Morgan sent two men to see if there was anyone in the outbuildings, then to watch out for any approaching riders.

The rest of them, with the two women at gunpoint, entered the house and searched the ground floor, where they found Carmen and Maria. Morgan told two men to stay there guarding the two Mexican women. He and the remaining two men went upstairs with Martha and Rebecca. They stopped in the passage outside the bedrooms. Morgan went ahead with gun in hand and looked in each room. In the last one he came to he found Clint and Jamie. Holding the gun on Clint, he beckoned to the others to join him in the bedroom. The helpless Clint stared at the three armed intruders, who were clearly holding his wife and mother prisoner.

'Now's the time for talking,' said Morgan. 'What we've come for is the boy.'

He pointed to Jamie, who was standing, wide-eyed, by the side of the bed on which his father was lying. Frightened, he was looking at the pistols in the hands of the three strangers.

'We're taking him with us,' Morgan went on, 'and listen good to what I'm going to tell you, because I ain't going to say it again. We figured that owning a big outfit like this, you'd be willing to pay well to get the boy back. The figure we fixed on is a hundred thousand dollars in used banknotes. We'll allow you a few days to get hold of this. Five days from now two men, no more, will leave here at daybreak to take the money into Mexico. They'll camp out overnight, and the following day they'll cross the Rio Grande some way downstream from El Paso at a ferry crossing called Brady's Crossing. Your men will arrive there around noon and they'll be met on the Mexican side.

As soon as we have the money the boy will be handed over.'

He paused as the sound of a shrill scream coming from downstairs was heard. He sent one of his men to investigate. Keeping a close watch on his prisoners, Morgan remained silent until the man returned.

'It was Snell,' the man reported. 'Seems he took a fancy to the young Mexican woman. I told him to keep her quiet.'

'Damn Snell,' said Morgan. 'Most of the time he just don't seem to be able to think of anything but women.'

He continued his talk to the prisoners. 'We'll be watching your men all the way,' he said. 'If we see any sign of a posse of lawmen coming after us, the boy dies. Any false moves on the part of your men, and the boy dies. The same thing happens if anybody follows us when we leave here.'

At a signal from Morgan one of his men took hold of Jamie and carried him, kicking and struggling, from the room. Morgan ordered the prisoners to stay in the room for the next fifteen minutes. Then he and his companions left, closing the door behind them. Downstairs, they saw Carmen sitting on a chair. She was dishevelled, blood was streaming down one side of her face, and she was sobbing convulsively. Maria was standing by the side of the chair, comforting her. Morgan told Snell and the man with him that they were leaving. Shortly after, all seven men rode off to the south with Jamie.

When Martha and Rebecca left the bedroom, Carmen was still sitting on the chair in a state of shock and distress, with Maria attending to her wound. They ran over to her and Rebecca stayed with her while Martha hurried to the bunkhouse. Inside, she found Bailey and Radford. Both hands had been shot dead. Lying by each of them was the gunbelt he had been about to buckle on when he was shot down. Martha ran back to the house.

'Rebecca,' she said. 'Ride out to Jacob at the roundup. I can tell you roughly where he'll be. Tell him what's happened here. Tell him to come here with Carmen's husband Juan, but nobody else. And tell him to send a rider to Doc Lloyd in Trasco to ask him to come to the ranch house right away to tend to Carmen.'

Rebecca left a few minutes later and Martha and Maria tended to Carmen. Three and a half hours passed before Rebecca returned with the rancher and Carmen's husband. Kennedy had already received a full account from Rebecca of events at the ranch house and bunkhouse. Leaving Maria with Juan and Carmen, the others went up to Clint in the bedroom. Rebecca, desperately worried about the welfare of Jamie, went to sit on the bed by her husband.

'We need to do some clear thinking here,' said the rancher, a bearded man in his late fifties, big and strong like his two sons. 'There's no doubt we're dealing with a bunch of killers with no spark of

11

human decency. We can't do anything to risk Jamie's life. So we need to keep the kidnapping quiet. I told none of the hands about it, except Juan. I don't see no option but to do exactly what they say. The money's no problem. We can have it ready in time.'

'You're right, Father,' said Clint, highly frustrated over his own enforced lack of mobility at such a crucial time. 'But who's going to take the money?'

'Naturally, I'll be one of them,' said Jacob Kennedy.

'We need to get Dan here,' said Martha. 'He'll know how best to handle this.'

'You're right,' said her husband. 'The two of us can take the money together. I'll telegraph him in Amarillo. I'll write the message now and take it to the telegraph office in Trasco myself. And while I'm there I'll ask the undertaker to come for the two bodies in the bunkhouse.'

He went downstairs to his desk. Martha went to sit with Carmen and Rebecca stayed in the bedroom with Clint, discussing the situation with him. She was close to tears.

The rancher was halfway to Trasco when he met Doc Lloyd in his buggy, heading for the Rocking K ranch house. The doctor was a long-standing friend of the family. Kennedy told him about the kidnapping, asking him to keep it to himself. He also told the doctor that, from Maria's account, one of the kidnappers, a man called Snell, had forced his attentions on Carmen. When she resisted, he had struck her savagely on the face, causing a deep cut on her cheek. Then he had brutally raped her.

'I'm going into Trasco now,' he went on. 'I'm telegraphing Dan to come and help us out. See what you can do for Carmen, Doc. Apart from anything else, I reckon that cut on her face is going to need a few stitches.'

They parted company and Kennedy rode on to the telegraph office.

TWO

The telegraph message sent to Dan Kennedy in
Amarillo read:

> JAMIE KIDNAPPED BY GANG OF SEVEN.
> ONE OF GANG NAMED SNELL. RANSOM
> MONEY TO BE HANDED TO THEM ON FAR
> SIDE OF MEXICAN BORDER BY SELF AND
> ONE OTHER SIX DAYS FROM NOW. IF LAW
> IS CALLED IN JAMIE DIES. NEED YOUR
> HELP. COME SOONEST. JACOB KENNEDY.

When Dan received the message at Ranger headquarters in Amarillo he immediately went to see
Ranger Captain Donovan. He asked for leave of
absence to help his family on the Rocking K with
some serious problems they were having.

'That's all right,' said the captain, certain that Dan
would not have asked for leave without proper justi-
fication. 'Come back as soon as the situation allows.

14

Is there anything we can do to help?'

'Thanks,' said Dan, 'but this is something we'll have to attend to ourselves. I aim to take the south-bound stage at midnight.'

Dan went to the bank to take out some cash. As he was leaving, he encountered Josh Brennan, a close friend of his, who had been retired from the Texas Rangers a month earlier. Josh was the son of a white father and a Kiowa woman. With his parents he had lived with the Indians until both his parents died. Then he had been taken on by the Rangers because of his tracking ability and fighting skills. He was a short, powerful man, still keen-eyed and surprisingly light of foot. Once, on an operation, he had saved Dan's life. On another occasion, Dan had returned the favour. Dan told him that he was about to leave Amarillo in response to a distress call from the Rocking K.

'This last few weeks,' said Josh, 'I've found mighty boring. I'm wondering if you could do with some help when you get to the ranch. I ain't *that* old yet.'

'It so happens, Josh,' said Dan, 'that you could be a big help to the family. But are you really sure you want to leave the comforts of retirement here in Amarillo for the dangers of facing a gang of seven outlaws?'

'I'm sure,' Josh replied.

'All right,' said Dan, and showed Josh the tele-graph message.

'I've heard or seen the name Snell somewhere

15

before,' said Josh. 'I think he's one of the Morgan gang who've been raising hell in Kansas and Colorado.'

'I'll check that up,' said Dan. 'I'm going to look through our files now. We'll leave on the midnight stage.'

Dan's search of the files was fruitful. He found information on a gang of seven outlaws led by a nan called Morgan and including one called Snell. He got copies of Wanted posters giving descriptions of all seven members of the gang. At midnight he boarded the southbound stage with Josh.

Dan had sent a message to the Rocking K giving the probable time of their arrival in Trasco, and when, after a long journey, they turned up there on schedule, Jacob Kennedy was waiting for them with two horses. They rode straight to the ranch house, and all the family members plus Josh assembled in Clint's bedroom. There, Dan and Josh were given a full account of the raid during which Jamie had been kidnapped.

Dan asked about Carmen's condition and Martha told him that she had needed several stitches in a wound on her face, and was still badly shocked. Dan then showed them the Wanted posters and it was confirmed that the gang involved was the Morgan gang.

'There are two things to think on,' said Dan. 'First, we've got to get Jamie back unharmed. But second, this gang has killed two loyal hands, both friends of the family over a lot of years. And Carmen has been brutally raped. We can't allow the gang to get away with this.'

Turning to his father he continued. 'I know, Father, that you're set on the idea that you and I should take the ransom money. But I have another idea. Josh here has been my partner for the last four years. He offered to help us out. He's the best tracker in the Ranger force working out of Amarillo. And in my opinion if he and I take on the job, this will give us the best chance of bringing Jamie back safe and sound.'

Grudgingly, the rancher nodded his head. 'I can see the sense in that,' he said.

'About the ransom money,' said Dan. 'I reckon that rather than carrying the money all the way from here, we should pick it up at the bank in El Paso, before crossing the Rio Grande at Brady's Crossing. D'you think that can be arranged?'

'I'm pretty sure there's enough time left to fix that,' said the rancher. 'I've been using the bank there for quite a while, as well as the one in Trasco. I'll put that in hand first thing in the morning.'

'Good,' said Dan. 'There ain't much more we can do now but wait till it's time for Josh and me to ride off.'

The rancher and his wife went downstairs with Josh, while Dan stayed to talk with Clint and Rebecca. He could see that they were both deeply worried about Jamie.

17

'What are the chances of getting Jamie back safe, Dan?' asked Clint.

'I just can't say,' said Dan. 'All I *can* say is that Josh and me will do our darnedest to make that happen.'

On the morning stipulated by Morgan Dan and Josh left the Rocking K and headed in the direction of El Paso. Several times during the day they both caught sight of the rider, some distance off to the right, who was following a path parallel to their own. They were pretty sure the rider was one of Morgan's men.

As night was approaching they made camp on a short stretch of flat ground scattered with boulders. They lit a campfire and sat down to take some food and drink.

'I have a feeling,' said Dan, 'that we can expect visitors before long.' Just over two hours later they had finished the meal and were sitting chatting by the fire. During a break in the conversation, Josh stiffened and listened intently.

'There are men moving out there,' he said, quietly.

'Don't move yet,' said Dan, 'but be ready for trouble.'

Minutes later they heard a call from a man out of sight in the darkness.

'Hello the camp,' he shouted. 'I'm coming in.'

Dan and Josh stood up. 'Come in with your hands raised,' shouted Dan.

A man appeared out of the darkness, holding his

18

hands up, and walked slowly towards them. As he drew closer to the fire, Dan and Josh identified him as Morgan, the leader of the gang. Morgan stopped a few paces away from them.

'I know you're from the Rocking K,' he said, 'and *you* know that the boy dies if harm comes to me or any of my men. So you might as well put those guns back in their holsters. Then I'll call my men in.'

Dan and Josh complied and Morgan shouted an order to his men. Five outlaws, each of them holding a pistol, walked up out of the darkness and formed a circle around Dan and Josh.

'Now, first of all,' said Morgan, 'I'd like to know who you two are.'

'I'm Dan Kennedy, son of Jacob Kennedy,' said Dan, 'and my partner here is one of the ranch hands.'

Keeping the two prisoners covered, Morgan gave an order to his men.

'Find the money,' he said, and watched while they carried out an exhaustive search of the campsite. But the money could not be found.

Enraged, Morgan spoke to Dan. 'You were supposed to bring the money with you,' he said. 'You'll both die for this. And the boy too.'

Dan took an envelope out of his vest pocket and handed it to Morgan.

'Maybe you should read this,' he said.

Morgan took a letter from the envelope and studied it closely by the light of the fire. While he was

19

doing this, Dan and Josh looked at the five men with him. They could identify all of them as members of the Morgan gang.

The letter was addressed to a bank manager in El Paso. It read:

Confirming telegraph message, please hand over to the bearer of this letter the sum of one hundred thousand (100,000) dollars in used banknotes. The bearer of the letter is my son Dan Kennedy whom you know personally.

The letter was signed by Jacob Kennedy.

'The bank in El Paso is the one my father mostly uses,' said Dan. 'The only way we could get the money to you in time was by picking it up in El Paso before we crossed the Rio Grande.'

'All right,' said Morgan, 'but once you've collected the money, follow the instructions I gave your people at the Rocking K. I don't want no more surprises. We'll see you in Mexico.'

A few minutes later Morgan and his men walked off to rejoin their horses and ride away from the camp. As they heard them leaving, Josh and Dan quickly saddled their mounts.

'You'll have noticed,' said Josh, as they were doing this, 'that one of the gang was missing. He'll be guarding Jamie. Let's follow Morgan and the others. They may lead us to the boy.'

'That's what I'm hoping,' said Dan, as they rode

out of camp.

He had already had the experience of observing Josh's acute sense of hearing which enabled him to follow riders in the dark; his ability to follow the faint tracks of men and horses which were invisible to others, and his skill in moving up, like a shadow in the dark, on some unsuspecting human target.

They followed the riders, as far behind as was possible without the risk of losing them. They had covered about six miles in a south-westerly direction, when Josh came to a halt and listened for a short while.

'They've stopped,' he said. 'I'll go ahead on foot and see what's happening. I'll get back as soon as I can.'

Josh returned forty minutes later. He told Dan that the first things he had noticed were that the outlaws had not bothered to station a guard and that there were only six horses on the picket line.

'They're staying overnight in the remains of an old fort,' he said. 'There's only one building left standing, and all six men we've been following are in there. I stood by a hole where a window used to be. Morgan was talking about the operation, and I picked up some mighty useful information. Jamie is with one of the gang called Naylor somewhere near the far side of Brady's Crossing. Morgan and the others will join them tomorrow morning, and Morgan plans to take the money from us and then hold us and the boy to squeeze some more money

21

out of your father.'

'Right,' said Dan. 'Time's running short, but we've got to try and rescue Jamie from Naylor before the rest of the gang gets there. We'll head straight for the crossing.'

Riding as quickly as possible, they reached the ferry well before dawn. They roused Brady, who owned and operated the ferry. Dan convinced him of their need to cross immediately to the far side of the river, and offered him a large bonus for his co-operation. Brady dressed and as he led them to the ferry Dan asked him if a man with a small boy had crossed over recently.

'About three days ago, there was a man crossing with a boy sitting on the horse in front of him,' said Brady. 'It struck me the boy didn't look too well.'

Dan and Josh helped Brady pull the ferry to the opposite bank of the river. Then Dan spoke to him again.

'We're looking for the man and the boy,' he said. 'We think the man is hiding with the boy somewhere near the far side of this ferry. Can you think of any good hiding-places over there, not far from the river?'

Brady thought hard before replying. 'The best place I can think of,' he said, 'is a wide steep-sided ravine about half a mile south of the ferry landing. It's just off the main trail leading south. The sides are rocky, and riddled with nooks and crannies. That would be the place, I reckon.'

As Dan and Josh left the ferry they thanked Brady. Then they headed for the ravine. They found it without difficulty, and stopped at the entrance.

'Better let me walk on alone,' said Josh. 'The sky's starting to lighten up. I'll walk along and look for sign. If Naylor is in there, he'll probably be somewhere near this end of the ravine.'

Twenty-five minutes later Josh returned. 'We're in luck,' he said. 'About seventy yards along the ravine, on the left side, there are the footprints of a man and a boy. And there are signs that a horse has been led up the side of the ravine. Let's go and see if we can locate them.'

They moved along the ravine, and Josh showed Dan the point from which the horse had been led up the slope. In the growing light Josh followed the horse tracks. Halfway up the slope they passed through a recess in the wall of the ravine. Following them, Josh stopped suddenly as he caught sight of a horse standing at the back of the recess, out of sight of the bottom of the ravine. In the side of the recess was the narrow entrance to what looked like a cave.

Josh could hear no sounds from inside. Whispering to Dan to stay where he was, Josh moved close enough to the cave entrance to see the footprints of a man and a boy going in and out. He returned to Dan, and they withdrew a little way down the slope.

'I'm sure they're both in there,' said Josh.

'We can't risk going into the cave,' said Dan.

'Naylor might shoot Jamie if we do. But I have an idea. We know that Morgan and the others will be coming here this morning. I'm going to ask you to carry out the hardest part of the plan because I know you can do it better than me.'

'What d'you have in mind?' asked Josh.

Dan explained his plan, then Josh made his way, out of view of anyone inside the cave, to a smaller recess in the back of the one in which the cave was located. Dan moved to a crevice close to where he was standing, where he would be hidden from Naylor should the outlaw look down the slope.

Dan waited a short while to make sure that Josh was in position. Then he leaned out of the crevice, and several times, as loudly as he could, he shouted,'Hello Naylor.' Then he drew back out of sight.

Inside the cave, Naylor was lying awake, thinking of rising and taking breakfast. He was a big man with a hard, brutal face, disfigured by a scar on one cheek. Jamie was lying on the floor, tied hand and foot, with his arms bound to his sides.

Naylor stiffened as he heard the shouting outside. He was expecting Morgan and the others to turn up sometime that day, but he was not hearing the password which had been agreed. He rose, checked his six-gun, and took hold of the rope around Jamie's chest. He dragged the boy outside. Then, holding Jamie in front of him, with a pistol in his left hand pointing at the boy's head, he moved to a point from which he could look down the slope into the bottom of the ravine.

He stood there, but could see no sign of the caller. Dan called several more times from his hiding-place, and Naylor, looking up and down the ravine, tried to locate the caller. Behind him, Josh left his hiding-place and moved up silently behind Naylor. With his left hand he knocked the pistol upwards, away from the boy's head. With his right hand he plunged his knife deep into the outlaw's back. The pistol went off but the shot flew wide. At the sound of the shot Dan stepped out from his hiding-place.

Naylor collapsed, releasing Jamie who, before Josh could grab him, started sliding and rolling down the rocky slope. Bound as he was, he faced severe injury before he reached the bottom some way below.

Desperately, Dan scrambled sideways across the slope. He arrived just in time to arrest Jamie's fall and grab hold of him. For one chilling moment he teetered on the point of losing his balance and falling down the slope with Jamie. But he recovered and carried the boy up to where Josh was standing. He looked down at Naylor.

'Dead,' said Josh. 'He was holding a gun to Jamie's head.'

Dan laid the boy down and took off the ropes. During the short fall he had suffered only minor cuts and bruises on his head and hands. Understandably shaken by his recent ordeal, he was near to tears.

'It's all over, Jamie,' said Dan. 'Soon you'll be back

with your mother and father. Did the men hurt you at all?'

'No,' said Jamie, 'but they kept me tied up most of the time.'

He rose to his feet. 'Where are the other men now?' he asked, apprehensively.

'Not far away I think,' said Dan, 'which is why we need to leave here pronto.'

Hastily, they left Naylor where he was and led his horse down the slope to the bottom. Dan lifted Jamie on to the horse, then he and Josh went to pick up their own mounts. Looking towards the ferry they could see no sign of riders. They rejoined Jamie, and all three rode on through the ravine to the far end. There they halted for a moment.

'What we're going to do now, Jamie,' said Dan, 'is circle round so we can cross the river at El Paso. This should keep us clear of the outlaws. We'll send a message to your mother and father from El Paso. Then we'll head straight for the Rocking K. And when we've got you back home I'm going to see what I can do about catching up with those other men who took you away from the ranch.'

'Myself, I aim to stay around here,' said Josh. 'If we lose touch with the gang it could take a long time to find them again. I aim to follow them. As soon as they've settled down in one place I'll send you a message at the Rocking K, and you can join up with me.'

'Now that we've got Jamie back,' said Dan, 'are you

sure you want to carry on helping me, Josh? It's going to be mighty dangerous from now on. There are still six outlaws to deal with.'

'I'm sure,' said Josh. 'Those men have murdered and raped and come mighty close to killing a young boy. We can't let them stay free. We'll work together. And maybe we'll be able to get the law to help us out.'

'All right,' said Dan. 'I'll wait at the ranch for your message.'

While Dan and Jamie rode on to El Paso Josh sought a vantage point from which he could safely observe developments when the body of Naylor was discovered by the gang.

The message from Dan to the Rocking K saying that Jamie was safe and well gave rise to great relief and joy. When they arrived at the ranch Dan told the full story of the rescue. Then he said that he was going to join Josh as soon as he heard from him, to deal with the remaining six members of the gang. Later, when he went to his room he took out the seven Wanted posters, selected the one relating to Naylor, and tore it into small pieces.

On the day that Jamie was rescued from the ravine, Morgan and five of his gang were waiting near the Mexican side of Brady's Crossing at the time stipulated for the arrival of Dan and Josh. But they waited in vain. When they were one hour overdue Morgan left three men behind and rode to the ravine with the remaining two. Naylor's body was soon discovered and it became clear that the boy had been taken away.

'Damnation!' said Morgan, completely taken aback by the total failure of an operation which had appeared to be on the verge of success. 'I'm guessing that Kennedy's son and the man with him are responsible for this. There's nothing to stop them calling the law in now. We'd better hightail it to the hideout.'

They all rode back to the ferry and joined the other three men. They could see that there was no one waiting on the Texas side. They crossed and rode quickly off to the east.

From his vantage point at the top of one side of the ravine Josh had observed the movements of Morgan and the others. Half an hour after the gang had crossed on the ferry, he did the same.

THREE

Seven days after he arrived at the Rocking K with Jamie Dan received a message from Josh. It read:

> M AND OTHERS LOCATED NEAR LARIBO WEST OF SAN ANTONIO. STAY CLEAR OF LARIBO. WAIT FOR ME AT RIVER CROSSING ON TRAIL RUNNING EAST FROM LARIBO ONE MILE OUT OF TOWN. BRING PROVISIONS.
> JOSH.

Dan showed the message to his father and the others and told them he would be leaving within the hour.

'With Josh's help,' he said, 'I aim to put this gang right out of business.'

'You two take care,' said his mother. 'We'll be waiting to hear from you.'

When Dan rode within sight of Laribo, there were

still two hours to go before nightfall. He half-circled the town and rode along the trail to the east. He crossed a small river about a mile from town, dismounted, and sat down to take a meal. Half an hour later, he saw a rider approaching him from the east. It was Josh. He dismounted as he reached Dan.

'Figured you'd be getting here about now,' he said.' I was watching out for you from some high ground back there.'

'I reckon,' he went on, 'that I've found the place where the Morgan gang hides out most of the time between jobs. It's a medium-size cattle ranch called the Circle Dot. The ranch house is about ten miles north east of here. I followed the gang all the way from Brady's Crossing and saw them go into the ranch house. And I'm pretty sure they haven't left the ranch since. I rode into Laribo one day after dark and had a talk with the liveryman. Pretended I was looking for work. He told me the Circle Dot was owned by a man called Carling, and that he and his hands, about ten of them, rode into town now and then.'

'I wouldn't be surprised,' said Dan, 'if the real owner of the ranch was Morgan. It's a perfect hideout for the gang. And likely he's paying the ordinary ranch hands enough to keep their mouths shut if they happen to suspect what's going on.'

'I reckon you're right,' said Josh. 'What's our next move? Do we get in touch with the Texas Rangers at San Antonio?'

'I know for a fact,' said Dan. 'that they're tied up now investigating some large-scale cattle-rustling, with stolen cattle being driven over the Mexican border. It could be quite a while before they could send a posse here, and by then the gang could have left on some operation. I reckon we're on our own for the time being. I expect you've found a good hiding-place overlooking the ranch buildings?'

'There's some high ground not far from the ranch house,' said Josh. 'I found a good place there. I'll take you there now.'

They rode off into the gathering darkness and Josh led the way to the high ground on one side of the big valley in which the ranch was located. They rode down into a hollow, deep enough to hide them and their horses from anyone in the valley below. From the rim of the hollow there was a clear view in all directions. Josh pointed out the faint lights coming from the Circle Dot buildings.

'During daylight,' he told Dan, 'there's a lookout stationed on a covered platform on the roof of the house. I've seen them through the field glasses, climbing up there. The guard's changed every four hours. And when I went down there after dark last night to take a look round, there was a guard posted outside the house. I got pretty close to him, and when he struck a match to light a cigarette, I could see he looked mighty like the one called Snell. So it looks like the men from the gang could be covering the night watch.'

'That gives me an idea,' said Dan. 'It would be crazy for the two of us to try and capture all six at the same time. We could try capturing one at a time. Then I could take the prisoner to the nearest jail, while you kept watch on the others till I got back.'

'That sounds a good idea to me,' said Josh. 'When do we start?'

'Tonight, after midnight, would be a good time,' said Dan.

Before they left at one in the morning, they removed all traces of their presence from the hollow. They stopped short of the ranch buildings and dismounted.

'I'd better go on alone,' said Josh. 'Come in when I give the coyote call.' Moving like a shadow in the night he checked the outsides of the buildings. He soon established that only one guard had been posted, and he was outside the house near the front door. After peering round the corner, Josh quickly withdrew as he heard the door of the house open and a man came out to relieve the guard. After a brief interchange of words the one who had been relieved went inside. Josh could see that the other one was now patrolling slowly up and down along the front of the house.

Josh waited till the man's back was turned to him. Then he ran up silently behind him and struck him on the head with the barrel of his pistol. He collapsed without a sound and before he could come round Josh had gagged him and bound his hands and feet with rope he had carried with him. He called out to Dan, who came and helped him carry their prisoner to the horses.

'The guards have just changed over,' Josh told Dan, 'so we should have over three hours to get well away from here before this man is missed. Wait here with him while I get a horse from that fenced-in pasture near the barn.'

Waiting for Josh, Dan struck a match and looked at the face of the prisoner, who was coming to. Relieved, he saw that it was Snell, one of the men they were after. When Josh returned with the horse Dan told him the identity of the prisoner and they hoisted Snell across the horse's back, secured him there, and headed towards San Antonio. Josh selected a route which would make their tracks impossible to follow continuously.

They had covered around fifteen miles when they rode into a small gully and dismounted. The prisoner was pulled off the horse and dropped on the ground. Dan and Josh walked out of Snell's hearing. It was almost daybreak.

'We should be all right here for a while,' said Dan. 'We don't know how Morgan's going to react to Snell's disappearance. They'll soon find that a horse is missing. He'll probably suspect that Snell's been taken away against his will. And maybe he'll think we have something to do with it. He could decide that the gang should leave the Circle Dot for a while.'

'I'll ride back there after dark,' said Josh, 'and I'll

find out what's happening. If the gang leaves before you get back, we'll follow their tracks.'

'All right,' said Dan. 'I'll arrange to reach San Antonio with Snell after dark today. What with his sore head and travelling slung over the back of a horse, I reckon it's mighty uncomfortable for him. But that don't bother me one bit, not after what he did at the Rocking K.'

Dan rode off later with Snell, after arranging to meet Josh at the hollow on the Circle Dot after dark the following day. He reached San Antonio after nightfall. He was familiar with the town, having been stationed there with the Rangers for a spell. He rode up to the rear of the building housing the office of Texas Ranger Captain Harrison and the jail cells. Leaving Snell on the horse, he walked round to the front and went inside. There he found Ranger Greeley, with whom he had been friendly. Greeley was surprised to see him.

'We've only just heard,' he said, 'about you and Josh rescuing your nephew from the Morgan gang. What in blazes are you doing here?'

Dan explained that he had one of the Morgan gang round the back, and that he would like him to be put in a cell without the townsfolk being aware of this.

'Let's bring him in through the back door,' said Greeley. 'Then I'll go for the captain. You'll remember his house is close by.'

They carried Snell into a cell, took the ropes off

him, and left him there. Dan waited in the office while Greeley went for the captain. When he returned with Harrison, Dan told them both about recent events, and handed over the Wanted notice he had been carrying that related to Snell.

'Snell is the man I just brought in,' he said. 'He's the one who raped the wife of one of the hands at the Rocking K. But I'd like it kept quiet for a little while that he's in jail here. It might help us if Morgan doesn't get to know that. I'd like to keep him guessing.'

'There's no problem with that,' said Harrison. 'Judge Benson is sick right now. It'll be a while before Snell is tried. Tell Josh Brennan that he's reinstated as a Texas Ranger for this operation. And I'll let Captain Donovan in Amarillo know what the two of you are doing down here. You'll be going after the gang again?'

'That's right,' said Dan. 'I'm due to meet Josh tomorrow after dark at a spot overlooking the Circle Dot buildings.'

'Right,' said the captain. 'I've no men to spare right now to help you out, but keep me posted about the situation.'

Dan left San Antonio the following day and rode into the hollow on the Circle Dot an hour after nightfall. But the hollow was deserted. There was no sign of Josh. Dan settled down to wait in the expectation that Josh would turn up before long.

*

After Dan had left the gully with Snell for San Antonio, Josh stayed on there for a while. Then he rode off towards the Circle Dot. He was about ten miles from the ranch house when, as he was breasting a rise, he saw a group of riders ahead of him, some distance away. He dismounted and led his horse back out of sight of the riders. Then he lay down and watched them through field glasses as they drew closer.

There were five riders in all. One of them was riding a pinto, very similar to the one Morgan was riding when Josh had last seen him on a horse. As they drew even closer, Josh became more and more convinced that he was looking at the five remaining members of the Morgan gang. They were following a route which would take them over the rise some distance away from Josh. He led his horse down the slope and into a small group of trees at the bottom. From there he observed the group as they rode down the rise and continued on their way.

Night was fast approaching and Josh decided to follow the riders in the hope that soon they would stop and make camp for the night. This would give him the chance to confirm that they were the Morgan gang. Also, he might be able to find out what place the gang was heading for. If he was lucky enough to achieve this he could go and collect Dan at the hollow the following day, before heading straight for the gang's destination. If not, he would go for Dan and they would follow the tracks of the horses.

He shadowed the gang for three miles, then saw them ride into a small gully, from which they did not emerge. He guessed they intended to camp there for the night. He waited until darkness had fallen. Then he secured his horse seventy yards from the gully and advanced on foot. He soon discovered that no guard had been posted. He looked down into the gully from the top of one of the sides. Down the gully a campfire had been lit and men were seated on the ground close by it.

Josh moved along until he was level with the campfire, which was close to the wall of the gully, almost vertical at this point. He lay down with his eyes just clear of the edge and surveyed the scene below. Five men were seated near the fire, which was burning brightly. One by one, Josh recognized them as the five men he and Dan were after. The men had just finished a meal and were talking together. But Josh could barely hear what they were saying.

In an effort to hear better he rose to his knees, then moved forward a little so that when he lay down again his head would be in a better position to hear the conversation below. But before he could lower himself, the thin layer of rock between his knees and the underside of a slight overhang beneath them gave way. Taken completely by surprise, Josh plunged downwards, striking his head on the hard wall as he fell. Stunned, he landed on the ground close to the fire, almost hitting two of the outlaws. A minute later, when he came to, his gun and knife had been removed and he was lying on the ground surrounded by the outlaws.

Morgan told three of his men to look for Josh's horse outside the gully and make sure there had been nobody with him. Then he looked at Josh, who was now sitting up, conscious of the calamity which had befallen him. Morgan had recognized Josh as the man who had been accompanying Dan to help recover Jamie after the kidnapping.

'You've dropped yourself into a whole heap of trouble here, spying on us like that,' he said. 'Now we can find out what's happened to my man Snell, the one you and your partner took from the Circle Dot. And we'd like to know where your partner is, as well. I know a lot of ways we can get this information out of you. But not here. It'll have to wait a little while.'

He held a gun on Josh while the other man tied him hand and foot. Shortly after this the three men came back into the gully, leading Josh's horse. They told Morgan that all the indications were that Josh had been alone.

During the night two outlaws were on guard, one watching Josh, the other guarding the entrance to the gully. Josh slept only fitfully, wondering what the following day had in store for him.

FOUR

When Josh had not turned up at the hollow by day-break on the day following his own arrival there, Dan decided he would stay there until two hours after nightfall in the hope that Josh would turn up before then. He spent all day watching the Circle Dot buildings. The only thing of interest that he noted was that there did not seem to be a lookout stationed on the roof of the house. This, he thought, could be an indication that the Morgan gang had left.

During the two hours after nightfall he grew more and more concerned about Josh's absence. He had a premonition that his friend was in trouble He decided to pay a visit to the Circle Dot to see if he could find out whether the Morgan gang was still there, and whether he could pick up any information which would account for Josh's non-appearance at the hollow.

When he arrived there, he dismounted well away from the buildings and approached them cautiously on foot. He could see no sign of guards. The call was given for supper and he watched from a distance as the hands entered the cookshack. Then he approached a side wall of the house. A light was showing through one of the windows. He walked up to this and peered through a gap in the curtains. He could see two men seated at a table, taking supper. Neither of them was a member of the Morgan gang. He assumed that one of them was Carling, who ran the ranch, the other possibly his foreman. The window was closed, so he was unable to listen to their conversation. He noticed that the table was close to the foot of a flight of stairs which presumably led to the sleeping accommodation.

He looked up at a window on the floor above. A ladder, fixed to the side of the house to give access to the lookout platform, ran close to this window. He climbed up the ladder. The top half of the window was open a little and he pushed it right down. He climbed through into the bedroom, left the room and went along the passage to the head of the stairs. Crouching there, he could hear the conversation at the table.

What he heard over the next fifteen minutes was of no interest whatsoever to Dan. Then he pricked up his ears.

'I'm sending a telegraph message to Morgan,' Carling was saying. 'I'm going to write it now. I want you to take it to the telegraph office in town early tomorrow. Be there when the office opens. I'll leave

40

the message on my desk. You can pick it up from there in the morning.'

Dan heard Carling's companion leave the house. He went back to the room which he had entered from outside, pulled the blind down, and looked round it with the help of matches. It was obviously not in use. He raised the blind and then the window to their former positions. He decided to stay in the room until Carling had retired for the night. He stood against the wall, near to the door.

He had been waiting a little over two hours when he heard a sound in the passage outside. He saw, under the door, the light from the lamp which Carling was carrying. Then he heard the sounds of the door to the next room opening and closing as Carling went inside. When sounds of movement in the next room had ceased he waited a further half-hour before moving silently downstairs. He found a lamp standing on a table and lit it, turning the flame down low. He moved to the desk standing in a corner of the room.

Lying on top of the desk was an unsealed envelope. He pulled out a sheet of paper on which Carling had written a message. It was addressed to *Will Hamlin, Saloonkeeper, Tremona, Texas.* The message read: *Message received from Fort Worth. Advising shipment from Fort Worth end of month has been postponed 4 or 5 weeks. Date will be advised. Carling Circle Dot, Laribo, Texas.*

Dan committed the message to memory. Then he

carefully put the paper back in the envelope and laid the envelope on the desk. He went to the door leading outside. It was locked and the key was hanging on a hook close by. He guessed that the man who had been eating with Carling had another key. To avoid suspicion that an intruder had been in the house during the night he figured he should leave by the way he had entered.

He extinguished the lamp, returned it to its former position, and went back upstairs. He left through the bedroom window, pulling it up behind him. When he reached his horse he stood for a short while, thinking about the message he had just read. He suspected it contained information relating to a planned robbery by the Morgan gang, either from a stagecoach or a Wells Fargo express wagon. He had never been to Tremona, but he knew it was a small town a good distance away, in the direction of Fort Worth. He rode back to the hollow, in case Josh had turned up there during his absence. But there was no one there. He decided to head for Tremona, reasoning that Josh had either been captured by the gang or had followed them. He must get there as quickly as possible.

He rode through the rest of the night and up to nightfall the following day, taking short breaks from time to time. He camped for the night and rode on the following morning. It was in the afternoon, when he judged he was not far from his destination, that on the trail ahead he saw two men and a woman standing by their horses in the sweltering heat. He rode up to them and dismounted, tipping his hat to the woman. The men were both armed and obviously not cowhands or homesteaders. They were both in their thirties, well built, with an arrogant look about them. Their names were Fender and Hall. They both scowled at the stranger.

Dan looked at the woman. She was slim, auburn-haired and attractive, probably in her mid-twenties. Her face was flushed. She looked closely at Dan, and felt instinctively that this was a man she could trust. She spoke to him.

'I'd be obliged,' she said, 'for a ride into Tremona. My horse stumbled back there and damaged a foreleg. It's not serious but I can't risk riding her there. I'll have to lead her to town.'

Fender cut in before Dan could reply. 'Just get back on your horse, stranger,' he said, 'and ride on before you gets hurt. We can take care of the lady. She can ride double with either one of us.'

The woman cut in. 'I'm mighty tired of you two bullies hassling me,' she said. 'I don't like you. The last thing I'd ever want to do is ride with either one of you. But I don't want to get a stranger into trouble. I'll walk into town with my horse, alone.'

'Not a good idea,' said Dan, ' 'specially in this heat. It would pleasure me to have your company into town. But first, let's make it clear to these two that we don't want them getting in the way.'

The two men bridled. Fender was a crooked

gambler employed by Hamlin, the owner of the saloon in Tremona, to boost profits from the gambling side of the business. He fancied himself as a shootist and had been involved in several fatal gun duels with poker players who had accused him of cheating. Hall was also employed by Hamlin in the saloon. His job was to eject any drinkers or disgruntled gamblers who were causing trouble. The two men walked clear of the woman and the horses and stood facing Dan.

'You've got a big mouth, stranger,' said Fender, his right hand hovering close to the handle of the six-gun in his holster. 'You had your chance to leave. This is where we teach you a lesson.'

He made a quick smooth draw which he fondly imagined would outdo that of the stranger. Dan scarcely seemed to move. But a pistol suddenly appeared in his right hand and was levelled and cocked before Fender had pulled back the hammer on his six-gun. The bullet from Dan's Peacemaker gouged a furrow in the flesh on Fender's arm, above the elbow. The gambler lost his hold on his six-gun and it fell to the ground. Shocked, he stood motionless, holding his arm and staring at Dan.

Hall made his move at the same time as his partner, but he was not noted for his gun-handling ability. Staring into the muzzle of Dan's pistol well before he was ready to fire, he froze, then let his gun fall to the ground.

'Time for both you men to leave,' said Dan, and

watched as they mounted their horses in silence and rode off, seething with anger, towards Tremona.

The woman, impressed by Dan's handling of the situation, introduced herself.

'I'm Ruth Dennison,' she said. 'My father owns the livery stable in Tremona. I'm obliged for your help.'

'Dan Kennedy,' said Dan. 'I'm heading for Tremona. Aim to spend a few days there. How far is it from here?'

'About three miles,' she said. 'Beyond that ridge over there.'

Dan picked up the two six-guns and put them in a saddlebag. Then he took the reins of the woman's horse and walked it a few paces.

'Guess you're right,' he said. 'The mare should be able to make it to town if we take it slow.'

He mounted his horse and helped Ruth up behind him. Then, leading her mount, they headed for Tremona.

Jack Dennison, standing outside the door of his livery stable, saw Dan and Ruth riding double towards him, leading Ruth's horse. He was a man of average height, normally cheerful and energetic, and well respected in the community. Concerned, he helped Ruth off the horse.

'This is Mr Kennedy, Father,' said Ruth, glancing over at the saloon, where she saw the horses of Hall and Fender. 'He just done me a real good turn. We'll explain inside. But would you take a look at my horse's foreleg first.'

They went inside the stable with the horses and Dennison examined Ruth's mount.

'Not serious,' he said. 'A few days' rest will fix it. I'll take care of this other horse, then see you in the house.'

Inside the house, which adjoined the stable, Ruth chatted with Dan while they awaited the arrival of her father. She told him that Fender had been pestering her for some time to strike up a relationship with him, an idea which held no appeal for her whatsoever.

When Dennison came in Ruth told him of her encounter with Fender and Hall, followed by Dan's intervention.

'They've gone too far,' said the liveryman angrily. 'I aim to talk to them about it. And I need to have a word with Hamlin as well.'

'I don't think that's necessary, Father,' said Ruth, fearing for his safety. 'Those two were cut right down to size, and Fender has a bullet wound in the arm to prove it. And as for Hamlin, you know he'd take no notice.'

Dan decided that he could safely take Ruth and her father into his confidence. He told them the full story, starting with the kidnapping of Jamie, up to his own recent encounter with Fender and Hall.

'That telegram shows that Hamlin is tied up with the Morgan gang,' he said, 'and I'm hoping he can lead me to them. I'm mighty worried about my friend Josh. I think maybe they've captured him and are hiding out somewhere around here.'

He produced the Wanted posters for the Morgan gang and showed them to Ruth and her father. But neither had seen any of the men portrayed on the posters.

'That telegraph message I talked about,' said Dan. 'I'm sure it was sent from Latigo yesterday morning. Did you notice Hamlin or any of his men riding out of town yesterday?'

They both shook their heads.

'Hamlin has a horse,' said the liveryman, 'as well as Hall and Fender. But they keep them in a stable behind the saloon. So they could have ridden out of town without either of us seeing them.'

'Luke Foster might know,' said Ruth. 'He's an old-timer. Has a shack along the street. I call in to see him now and again. He sits out on his porch most of the day. Sees most of what's going on around town. I'll go along there now and have a word with him.'

Ruth returned twenty minutes later. 'Luke didn't see Hall or Fender leave town yesterday,' she said, 'but he did see Hamlin ride off just after noon. Luke's shack is on the edge of town and he saw that when Hamlin left town he he turned and headed east in the direction of a rock outcrop. He watched Hamlin till he rode past the outcrop and out of sight.'

'Did he see him come back?' asked Dan.

'Yes,' replied Ruth. 'It was about three hours later. And Hamlin was riding back the same way he went out.'

'In the direction Hamlin was riding,' asked Dan, 'are there any towns or small settlements within fifteen miles or so?'

'Nothing I can think of,' said Dennison. 'It's pretty desolate country out there.'

'There is Mahoney's place,' said Ruth, 'but that's just a store, a pretty big one at that, standing out there on its own. We've often wondered how Mahoney manages to find enough customers to make it pay.'

'The gang could be hiding in a cave or ravine,' said Dan. 'I'm going to ride out in that direction after dark and see if I can locate them.'

'You'll need to ride south out of town,' said Ruth, 'then turn east and head for the outcrop. You should be able to see it against the night sky. But right now, I reckon we all need a good meal. You're welcome to join us. I'll get some supper on the go.'

As they chatted over supper, Dan felt an increasing attraction towards Ruth. He hoped to further their acquaintance when his present mission had been completed. After supper he thanked the liveryman and his daughter for their help and prepared to leave.

'We'll see you back in town?' asked Ruth, well aware of the risks Dan was taking, and concerned about his welfare.

'That's one thing I'm certain about,' said Dan, smiling. 'Can't say just when, but I'll sure be back.'

He left shortly after, following Ruth's instructions,

and soon saw the outcrop looming ahead of him in the darkness.

Back in town, Ruth was talking to her father. 'I'm real scared he won't get out of this alive.'

'I ain't blind,' said Dennison. 'I could see you both took a shine to one another. I think he's a good man. Let's hope he manages to finish the job he's taken on.'

Dan rode on, keeping the North Star on his left and investigating any possible hiding-places along the line he was following, and on either side of it. It was a slow process in the dark, and by the time he had reached a point about fifteen miles from Tremona, dawn was not far away. He decided to stay on until daybreak in the small gully which he had just checked.

When the sun rose, Dan climbed up the side of the gully and looked towards the east through his field glasses. In the distance he could clearly see a large cluster of buildings which he took to be Mahoney's store. He decided to ride to the store and see if any of the folks there had seen any sign of the Morgan gang. But just as he was about to lower the glasses he saw a rider leave and head in his direction on a path which would take him clear of the gully. There was something familiar about the rider and his horse. Dan went to a point from which he could watch the rider without being seen. As he drew close Dan could see that it was Hall, one of the two men he had confronted the previous day. Hall had, in fact, ridden out to the store the previous evening with another message for Morgan which was being passed on by Hamlin. He had stayed at the store overnight.

The sighting of Hall gave Dan reason to suspect that the Morgan gang might be hiding out at Mahoney's place. He decided to stay in the gully until after dark before paying a visit to the store. He settled down to wait, keeping the buildings under observation. He hoped that during the forthcoming night he would be able to find Josh, assuming he was still alive, and rescue him.

FIVE

When Josh was captured by the Morgan gang he was taken on the long ride to Mahoney's store. On the way there he was given no possible chance of escape. On arrival at the store, after its closure in the evening, Morgan told Mahoney that he and his men would like to stay there a week or maybe longer.

'I can manage that,' said Mahoney, 'but what about that prisoner you've got with you? I don't like the idea of holding anybody prisoner here. It makes me nervous. What if he escapes, or somebody comes looking for him?'

'Neither of those things is going to happen,' said Morgan. 'The man has some information that I want real bad, and I have a feeling it's going to take a while to get him to talk. But as soon as he does we'll kill him and get rid of the body.'

'All right,' said Mahoney, 'but I'll have to charge the same for him as I do for you and the others. There's a small storage shed just outside the back of the store that's empty just now. You can keep him there.'

'All right,' said Morgan. 'I expect you've noticed that Snell ain't with us. He went missing and the man we brought with us probably had something to do with it. Have you heard any reports of Snell being in the hands of the law?'

Mahoney shook his head.

'We're going to find out from our prisoner where his partner is and what's happened to Snell,' said Morgan. 'If we can't get him to talk tomorrow, we'll cut off his food and drink for a while to loosen his tongue.'

'So long as you keep him gagged while you're beating him up,' said Mahoney. 'You and your men are the only ones staying here just now, but I don't want any screams disturbing anybody calling in at the store.'

Josh was taken to the small shed. It was a newly constructed timber building, not yet in use. It had one door, provided with a stout padlock on the outside. There were no windows. The prisoner's legs were tied together and his hands were bound together behind him. To prevent him moving around inside the shed his hands were secured to one of the vertical posts to which the sides of the shed were fixed. Josh was left sitting up, with his back to the post. The door was slammed, the padlock fastened, and he was left alone to consider the extremely dire situation in which he found himself.

He was sure that by now Dan would suspect that he had been captured or killed by the Morgan gang, but he would have no idea of Josh's present whereabouts. Josh was so securely tied that he could see no possibility of escaping by his own efforts. And he guessed that whatever he said when Morgan interrogated him, he was fated to end up as a corpse hidden in an unmarked grave at some lonely spot.

Josh spent the night in extreme discomfort. The gang checked the shed at intervals to make sure that he was still properly secured. In the morning, after the gang had breakfasted, Morgan and two of his men, Anderson and Wright, went to the shed. They took off the rope round Josh's legs, released him from the post, and stood him up with his hands still tied behind him. Josh looked impassively at the three men as Morgan spoke to him.

'It's clear to me,' said the outlaw, 'that you and Kennedy rescued the boy and killed Naylor. Then you took another of my men, Snell, from the Circle Dot. What you're going to tell me, either the easy way or the hard way, is where is Kennedy now, and exactly what has happened to Snell.'

Josh knew that his only chance of prolonging his life, even for just a short while, was to withhold any information which might be useful to Morgan.

'Can't help you there,' he said. 'I don't have the answers to those two questions.'

'Maybe we can jog your memory,' said Morgan. 'If you've got anything to tell us, just nod your head.'

He tied a gag over Josh's mouth. Then he gestured to Anderson, a tall brawny man with a hard, cruel face. Anderson walked up to Josh and let loose a vicious barrage of punches to the head and body. As Josh sagged under the onslaught, Morgan and Wright stepped forward to hold him upright while the assault continued. But Josh showed no sign of willingness to speak, and when he was obviously unconscious Morgan ordered Anderson to stop. Josh collapsed on the floor. He was quickly secured as before and the gag was removed.

'We'll stop the food and drink,' said Morgan, 'and have another go at him tomorrow.'

Josh came round as they were leaving the shed. Several cuts on his face and body were bleeding and he was feeling the effects of the heavy blows which Anderson had rained on him. He guessed that it was only a matter of time before he would be subjected to a similar ordeal again.

His fears were realized when he received the same treatment the following day, but he stubbornly refused to give Morgan the information he badly wanted. Once again he was left in the shed, weak and in considerable pain.

On the day that Josh received his second beating, Dan was keeping the store under observation from his hiding place in the gully. His intention was to visit the store after dark to check whether Josh and the Morgan gang were there. Throughout the day he saw a number of riders and buckboards calling at the store and then departing with their purchases.

He waited until after midnight, before riding towards the store. He secured his horse well away from the buildings and advanced on foot. He could see no lights showing from inside any of the buildings. He walked through a narrow gap between two of the buildings into an open central area. Cautiously, he moved around until he found the stable. He went inside, closed the door behind him, and lit an oil lamp which was hanging on the wall just inside the door. Carrying the lamp he took a close look at the nine horses inside the stable. First he found Josh's horse, which he could positively identify. Then he saw a pinto which he was almost sure was the one belonging to Morgan. So it seemed that Josh had been captured by the Morgan gang, and could still be alive. If so, he must find out just where he was being held. He extinguished the lamp and left the stable. He decided to walk round the perimeter of the central area, looking at the other buildings. The first one he approached was the store itself. As he passed a small shed standing clear of the main buildings, he heard faint sounds coming from inside it. He stopped and put his ear against the wall. He heard groans and the faint sounds from movements inside as Josh tried to find a position which would ease his pains.

Dan moved round to the door and could feel the stout padlock which was holding it closed. The possibility dawned on him that Josh was being held prisoner in the shed. He felt the bottom of the door. There was a small gap between it and the ground. He lay down with his mouth close to the gap and spoke in a low voice.

'Is that you in there, Josh?' he asked. 'This is Dan.'

There was silence for a moment, then Dan, with his ear close to the gap, heard the faint reply.

'I hear you, Dan,' said Josh. 'I'm all tied up in here. Watch out for somebody coming to check up on me. Could be any time now. Morgan and his gang are all staying here.'

Dan heard a door open somewhere nearby. Then he saw that a man carrying a lantern was walking towards the shed. He rose quickly and moved behind the shed, out of sight of the approaching man. As the outlaw came up to the door, he hung the lantern on a hook near to the padlock and felt in his pocket for the key. Peering along the side of the shed, Dan had a clear view of his face, illuminated by the lantern. He recognized him instantly as Anderson, a member of the Morgan gang.

Dan knew that if he and Josh were to escape, Anderson must be prevented from shouting for help or firing off his six-gun. He backed away from the shed, then quickly circled around and came up to the outlaw from behind just as he was unlocking the padlock. He struck him hard on the head with the barrel of his six-gun and Anderson collapsed without a sound. As he fell, his head slammed hard against a heavy chopping block standing near the shed. Dan bent down over him to gag him, but the outlaw was not breathing. A quick check confirmed that he was dead.

Dan opened the door of the shed and placed the lantern on the floor inside. Then he dragged the body in and closed the door. Quickly, he removed the ropes from Josh's hands and legs, then helped his friend to his feet. He noted the wounds on Josh's head and face and the pain he was obviously experiencing in the upper part of his body. He guessed that he had undergone a severe beating.

'Anderson here is dead,' said Dan. 'We'd better move quick, Josh. Can you ride? I've just seen your horse in the stable here.'

'I can ride,' said Josh. 'Let's get moving before Anderson is missed.'

Dan handed him Anderson's six-gun. Then he extinguished the lantern and they quit the shed, leaving the body inside. Dan padlocked the door and put the key in his pocket as they walked to the stable. Josh stayed outside, watching for any signs of movement in and around the buildings, while Dan quickly saddled his horse. The animal was led out of the stable, through the gap between two buildings, and over to the point where Dan's horse was waiting. Dan helped Josh into the saddle and they headed for Tremona. Behind them Morgan and the remaining three members of his gang were sound asleep, blissfully ignorant of the shock awaiting them. A mile from the store the two riders paused while Dan spoke to Josh. He had earlier decided that it would have been suicidal for himself and the injured Josh to take on the rest of the gang at the store.

'I don't reckon,' he said, 'that Morgan is going to waste any time searching for us. He'll be too worried about saving his own skin. He and his men will leave the store as soon as they find you've escaped. I've got friends in Tremona and I figured we could go there to have the doctor take a look at you and get some food into you. But do you reckon you could come back here and start following the horse tracks left by Morgan and his men?'

'I reckon so,' said Josh, 'provided we get back there soon and there's no heavy rainfall in between. It won't be the first time I've been following the tracks of those particular horses. When we get back there we'll circle the store till I pick them up.'

Their progress was slow because of Josh's condition and it was well past daybreak as they rode into Tremona. Dennison the liveryman was just opening the door of the stable, and he saw them approaching. He called to Ruth inside the house. She ran out and, greatly relieved to see Dan safely back, she joined her father as he walked out on to the street to meet the two riders. The two horses came to a halt, and Ruth and her father could see the profusion of cuts and bruises on Josh's face.

'This is my friend, Josh Brennan,' said Dan. 'He ain't feeling too good right now. I'll get the doctor to take a look at him, then we'll take rooms at the hotel.'

Ruth looked at her father. He knew exactly what was in her mind. Smiling, he nodded his head.

'You'll do no such thing,' said Ruth. 'We have a spare bedroom with two beds. You can go there now while I slip along to Doc Emery's house and ask him to come and see to Mr Brennan.'

'I'm mighty obliged, ma'am,' said Josh. 'I've got to say I'm really looking forward to climbing off this horse and lying down for a spell.'

Dan dismounted and eased Josh off his mount. Then the liveryman took them to the bedroom, where they were joined shortly after by Ruth and the doctor. While Emery was tending to Josh, the others went to the living room. Dan told them what head happened since he left Tremona.

'I want to send some telegraph messages,' he said. 'I want to tell the Texas Rangers about Mahoney's store being used as a hideout for criminals, and about Anderson being killed. They'll also be interested to hear how Hamlin has been helping Morgan. Is the telegraph operator in town a man who can be trusted to keep the contents of these messages to himself? We wouldn't want Mahoney or Hamlin to know what's in them.'

'The telegraph operator is a good man,' said the liveryman. 'And what's more, he's a good friend of ours. You write the messages and I'll take them to him. I'll explain the situation.'

'All right,' said Dan. 'The other message I want to send is to my father Jacob Kennedy on the Rocking K to let him know how the chase is going.'

While Dan was writing the messages Ruth went to see if she could help the doctor in any way. In the message to Ranger Captain Harrison in San Antonio, Dan explained briefly what had happened at Mahoney's store and how Hamlin had been involved. He told the captain that he and Josh intended to follow Morgan and the three remaining members of his gang as soon as they were able to take up the chase. As he completed the messages Ruth came in with the doctor.

'Your friend has taken a real beating,' he said to Dan, 'but no bones have been broken. I reckon he feels easier now I've tended to the cuts and bruises and bandaged him up. What he needs is to take some food and drink and rest up for a few days. But he's talking about riding out of here tomorrow. Maybe you can change his mind.'

'No use in trying, Doc,' said Dan. 'Josh is a mighty stubborn man.'

'All right,' said Emery. I'll put new bandages on tomorrow, before you leave.'

When the doctor had departed Dan told Ruth and her father that he and Josh, who was recognized as a first-rate tracker, planned to follow the tracks of the gang leading away from Mahoney's store. He thanked them for their help. The liveryman departed with the telegraph messages and Ruth took

Josh some food and drink. Dan accompanied her to the bedroom and they sat with Josh while he took the meal. Then, leaving him to rest they returned to the living room.

'So you'll be leaving tomorrow,' said Ruth, worried about the dangerous mission on which this man, to whom she felt so strongly attracted, was engaged.

'That's right,' said Dan. 'Josh is set on it. It'll make his job of tracking the gang that much easier. This is a job I have to finish, but when it's all over I'd like to come back here and start courting you, provided you feel the same way about me as I do about you.'

Ruth smiled at him. 'There's no doubt in my mind,' she said, 'that you're the man for me. I'll be waiting.'

The liveryman returned to say that the telegraph messages had been sent. They all had a meal, then Dan went up to the bedroom for some much needed rest. Before lying down he took the Wanted poster relating to Anderson from the ones he was carrying with him. He tore it up into small pieces.

The following morning, after the doctor had attended to Josh, Dan and his partner rode off towards Mahoney's store.

SIX

At Mahoney's store, it was not until Wright went to check the prisoner four hours after Anderson died, that Anderson's body was found and it was realized that the prisoner had escaped, almost certainly with some outside help.

With Mahoney by his side, Morgan stared down at the third member of the gang that he had lost since kidnapping the Kennedy boy. It was clear that the gang would have to leave their present hiding-place, and the sooner the better. He told Mahoney that they would be leaving soon after daybreak.

Mahoney, incensed that Morgan had been the cause of such a calamity, knew that he would have to abandon, and soon, a highly successful operation with profits coming mainly from the high charges imposed for sheltering his criminal guests.

The Morgan gang left soon after daybreak, after burying Anderson not far from the store. They were heading in a northerly direction.

*

On the day following the Morgan gang's departure from Mahoney's store, Dan and Josh circled the buildings at a distance until Josh spotted the tracks of four horses, heading north. He studied them closely.

'I'm sure these are the tracks we're looking for,' he said. 'It seems like they've all stayed together. Let's see where the tracks lead us.'

They followed them all day, camped out overnight, and carried on the following morning. During the pursuit Dan had become increasingly impressed with Josh's tracking skills. They stopped about midday for a brief respite.

'I reckon, Dan,' said Josh, 'that we ain't far from Fort Worth, and it looks like that's where these tracks are heading.'

'That's interesting,' said Dan. 'I wonder if it's any-thing to do with that postponed shipment from Fort Worth that was mentioned in the telegraph message I saw at the Circle Dot?'

'Could be,' said Josh. 'If they're going to stay at Fort Worth or somewhere near by, they'll need a good hiding place. Let's hope we can find it.'

Two hours later they could see Fort Worth in the distance. When they joined one of the main trails into town it was no longer possible, even for Josh, to follow the tracks any further. They had been obliter-ated by the passage of horse-drawn vehicles and other riders.

'I reckon,' said Dan, 'that a talk with the Ranger Captain in Fort Worth could be useful. It's hardly likely the gang's hiding out in the middle of town. That would be too risky for them. So we'll ride in after nightfall and take a couple of rooms at the hotel. Then we'll get in touch with Captain Armstrong.'

When they rode into Fort Worth they left their horses at the livery stable, then took a couple of rooms at the hotel before going to Captain Armstrong's office, which was nearby. They had both met the captain briefly, on two occasions in the past. Inside the office they found Ranger Ewing, whom they had also met before. They gave him a brief account of the reasons for their visit.

'The captain's at home,' said Ewing, 'but I reckon he'll want to talk with you right now. I'll go for him. You two wait here.'

He returned ten minutes later with Armstrong, a big, bearded man and a respected law officer with many years' experience in the Texas Rangers. He listened with mounting interest as Dan and Josh gave an account of their pursuit of the gang.

'I heard about you rescuing the boy,' he said, 'and I heard from Captain Harrison in San Antonio about you handing Snell over to him. You'll be interested to hear that Snell's been tried and was due to hang this morning. So Morgan has lost three of his men to you. And now you say that what's left of the gang could be hiding out somewhere around here.'

'We lost their tracks just outside of town,' said Dan, 'and from a telegraph message I read at the Circle Dot I know that Morgan got a telegraph message from somebody in Fort Worth telling him that a shipment from Fort Worth, scheduled for the end of this month, had been postponed. But it didn't say what the shipment contained. It struck me that it might be a valuable shipment going by stagecoach or express wagon.'

'You could be right,' said the captain. 'More likely to be a Wells Fargo express wagon carrying a gold shipment, I'd say. Somebody in Fort Worth could be handing out information about shipments. Let's go and see Garner, the Wells Fargo manager here. His office is close by. He's usually there in the evenings. I've known him a long time. If there's a leak from his office, I'm sure he's not the one responsible for it.'

He left, accompanied by Dan and Josh. They found Garner alone in his office, and the captain introduced his two companions. Then he asked Garner whether a valuable shipment of any kind from Fort Worth had been planned for the end of the month and had then been postponed.

Garner, a short elderly man on the verge of retirement, looked startled.

'That's true,' he said. 'It was a gold shipment worth about one hundred thousand dollars. But how did you come to hear about it? It was supposed to be a secret.'

The captain gestured to Dan who told the

manager about the telegraph message and the probable presence of the Morgan gang in the vicinity.

'The message I saw,' said Dan, 'stated that the shipment would be postponed for three or four weeks. Has the date been fixed yet?'

'Not yet,' replied Garner, 'but it will probably be six or seven days from now. What I'm concerned about is the leak. Only one person apart from myself knew about the original date of the shipment and the probable length of the postponement. And that was Lynch, my assistant. He joined me about six months ago. It's a shock to think he could be in the pay of the Morgan gang.'

'This could be our chance to capture the gang,' said the captain, looking at Dan. 'You know the gang pretty well. I expect you've got some ideas on how we might go about that.'

'I have a plan that I reckon stands a good chance of working,' said Dan. 'It assumes that the gang has already been in touch with Lynch, so he knows that they are here. I figured that we could feed Lynch with false information that the shipment is due to leave Fort Worth say five days from today. Then we would keep him under constant surveillance, hoping that he'll lead us to the gang when he passes the information on.'

'That sounds good to me,' said the captain, turning to Garner. 'Are you willing to co-operate?'

'I sure am,' said the manager. 'The Morgan gang has robbed the company several times in the past.

Tomorrow morning I'll tell Lynch that the gold ship-ment is definitely scheduled to leave Fort Worth at around noon on the day you suggest. Lynch has the afternoon off tomorrow, so maybe you'll be in luck. Maybe he'll ride off with the news and lead you to the hideout.'

'Right,' said Dan. 'With the captain's agreement Josh and me will start watching Lynch tomorrow morning, day and night. Like Mr Garner says, maybe he'll go to the gang with the news. Or maybe one of the gang will come to him after dark. Does he live alone?'

'Yes,' replied Garner. 'In a small house near the edge of town.'

'Let's go ahead with what's just been suggested then,' said Armstrong. 'I'll make sure we have enough men to take on the gang at the hideout when the time comes.'

As he finished speaking, the door opened and Lynch came in. He was a short slim man, neatly dressed, and in his forties. Curious, he looked closely at Josh and Dan. Armstrong was a fairly frequent visitor to the office, but the two men with him were both strangers to Lynch.

'Sorry, Mr Garner,' he said. 'I forgot to take my reading glasses with me when I left.'

The manager nodded and Lynch collected the glasses from a drawer in his desk and departed.

'So now you've seen Lynch,' said Garner, to Dan and Josh. He went on to give them the exact location of Lynch's house. He told them that when Lynch left town for a ride he hired a horse from the livery stable.

'We can see the stable and your office from our hotel rooms,' said Dan. 'So during daylight one or other of us will keep a watch from there. After dark, we'll find another place where we can watch Lynch's house in case he gets a visit from the gang.'

Josh and Dan left soon after, and went to the hotel for a meal. Then they went to their rooms.

They breakfasted early, then Josh, still feeling the effects of his beating, rested while Dan watched the Wells Fargo office and the livery stable. He saw Lynch arrive at the office, followed not long after by Garner. At noon, Lynch left the office and walked towards his house. Fifty minutes later he reappeared on the street and went into the livery stable. Dan spoke to Josh, lying on the bed near by.

'Lynch just went into the livery stable,' he said. 'I'd best get moving.'

'You're sure you don't want me to come along?' asked Josh.

'I reckon I can follow him without being seen,' said Dan, 'and he's less likely to spot one rider than two. You rest up here till I get back.'

Looking out of the window, he saw Lynch come out of the stable and ride off in a southerly direction. He went to Armstrong's office to tell him that it looked like Lynch had taken the bait and that he was going to follow him. Then he hurried to the stable for his own horse, and rode out of town.

He was in time to see Lynch climb a rise about half a mile to the south east of town and disappear down the far side. He rode to the top of the rise and saw Lynch in the distance, heading straight for his destination with no reason to believe that he might be followed. Dan kept out of sight of the rider ahead and, about eight miles out of town, watching from cover, he saw him ride into a ravine and disappear from view. watching through field glasses, Dan saw him reappear half an hour later and ride in his direction. Quickly, Dan sought cover with his horse in a small grove of trees nearby. From there he watched Lynch as he rode past on his way back to town.

Dan decided it would be wise to wait in the grove until darkness fell before confirming that the Morgan gang was in hiding in the ravine. He was sure that a lookout would have been posted to watch out for approaching riders.

He waited until it was sufficiently dark, then left the grove and headed for the side of the, ravine, some way up from the point at which Lynch had entered it. Having secured his horse well back from the top of the sloping side, he moved forward until he could look down into the ravine. Near the bottom of the far side he could see a campfire with three men sitting near by. As he watched one of the men rose and walked down the ravine until he was out of sight. Five minutes later another man, smaller in size, appeared in view from down the ravine and sat with the others. Dan was fairly certain that he was looking at the Morgan gang. But he needed to make sure.

He climbed down the side of the ravine some way up from the fire, then cautiously approached it. He passed close to a picket line to which four horses were fastened. One of them, a pinto, was very like the horse which Morgan had been riding. He moved as close to the fire as he could without being seen and crouched behind a boulder looking at the three men. As Morgan lit a cigarette, his face was briefly illuminated, and Dan knew that without doubt he was looking at the leader of the gang. Retracing his steps he climbed out of the ravine and rode back to Fort Worth.

On his arrival there he went straight to Captain Armstrong's house and gave him the news.

'So now we have the chance,' said the captain, 'to put the gang completely out of business. We'll raid their camp around forty-eight hours from now. I'll have enough men available by then. I'll tell Garner in the morning.'

On his way to his room at the hotel Dan told Josh of the day's events and the forthcoming raid. He was relieved that his friend would have a little more time to recuperate.

Late the following afternoon, when Lynch finished work, he was passing the telegraph office on the way to his house, when the operator called him in. He asked him whether Garner was still in the Wells Fargo office.

'He left half an hour ago,' said Lynch. 'I don't know where he was going.'

'In that case,' said the operator, 'maybe you can help me to read this message he asked me to send to Wells Fargo headquarters when he called in thirty minutes ago. You know his handwriting ain't that good. There's a word here I just can't make out. It's the very last word in the message.'

'I know what you mean,' said Lynch, surprised that the manager had not, as usual, asked him to take the message to the telegraph office. 'I have trouble with his handwriting myself. Let me take a look at the message.'

The operator handed him a sheet of paper and he looked at the last word of the message and quickly decided that it was intended to read 'resume'. Curious, he glanced at the other contents of the message and quickly realised their import.

The message read:

FURTHER TO RECENT MESSAGE CON-CERNING SUSPECTED PRESENCE OF OUTLAW GANG IN AREA, EXPECT EARLY CAPTURE OF GANG AFTER WHICH SHIP-MENTS BY EXPRESS WAGON FROM FORT WORTH WILL RESUME.

Severely shocked, Lynch pretended to be strug-gling to decipher the last word while carefully reading the whole of the message and committing it to memory. Eventually he spoke. His voice was strained.

'I'm pretty sure,' he said, 'that "resume" is what that last word is meant to be.'

The operator thanked him and Lynch left the office, fighting to suppress a growing sense of panic. All the indications were that his association with the Morgan gang was known and that he had been used to pass false information to the outlaws. It was imperative that he ride out to the gang and warn them. He went to his house and collected all the personal belongings he could carry with him. Then he went to the livery stable for a horse and rode out of town. Dan and Josh, who had ceased their surveillance of Lynch, were not aware of his departure.

Morgan, seated at the campfire with two of his men, was surprised to see Lynch riding up the ravine towards him. He was shocked to learn about the telegraph message, realizing its implications. He told one of his men to go and tell the lookout to be extra watchful.

'I can't figure out,' he said, 'how Garner came to know that we're in the area.

'Those two strangers I saw talking with Garner and the Ranger captain might have something to do with it,' said Lynch.

'Can you describe those two?' asked Morgan.

'Sure,' said Lynch, and gave a fairly accurate description of Dan and Josh, adding that one of them showed signs of recent blows to the head and face.

'Damnation!' shouted Morgan. 'They were Kennedy and that partner of his. We've got to leave here pronto before that posse turns up. I'm tired of being trailed by those two. We'll ride up to the Red River and make out we're crossing into the Indian Territory. We'll hide our tracks. Then we'll pick a hideout in Texas where we'll be safe for a while. Then, before we plan another robbery, I'm aiming to hunt down Kennedy and his partner, and finish them off for good. They're responsible for me losing three of my men. But how about yourself, Lynch? What are you aiming to do?'

'I'm leaving here right now,' said Lynch. 'I'm heading for New Mexico Territory. I have kinfolk there. I'll stay with them for a while.'

His departure was followed, half an hour later, by that of Morgan and the others. They were heading north for the Red River.

SEVEN

Lynch's absence from town was not noticed until he failed to turn up for work in the morning. Armstrong was told and Lynch's house was found to be empty. Enquiries revealed that the telegraph operator had been seen calling Lynch into his office and that Lynch had ridden out of town shortly after. The operator explained why he had intercepted Lynch and he showed the captain the message which he had transmitted. Armstrong passed it to Dan and Josh to read.

'It's clear what's happened,' he said. 'The gang's long gone by now. And Lynch is probably with them. But I'll get a posse together and you two can ride out with them to the hideout.'

The posse left forty minutes later, and found the signs of a hasty departure from the hideout. Just outside the ravine Josh found the tracks of five horses leaving it and heading in a northerly direction. He estimated that the tracks were over twelve hours old.

'I reckon they're heading for the Red River to cross into the Nations,' said Dan.

Josh followed the tracks until darkness fell. They camped out overnight and continued the chase at daybreak. They reached the Red River some way west of Red River Station where trail herds from South Texas taking the Chisholm Trail to Kansas normally forded the river. The tracks indicated that the Morgan gang, with Lynch, had crossed into the Indian Territory at this point, and had therefore left the jurisdiction of the Texas Rangers.

Dan told the other members of the posse, who were returning to Fort Worth, that he and Josh were going to follow the gang in the Indian Territory. They parted company and Dan and his partner crossed the river. Josh started looking for horse tracks on the northern bank. He ranged a short distance east and west along the bank, but could not find any hoofprints left by the gang.

'They're doing their best to hide their tracks,' he said. 'There are two possibilities. Maybe they rode their horses along the shallows near the south bank, either east or west, then rode back into Texas. Or maybe they've done the same thing on the north side of the river, and ridden into the Indian Territory.

'We'll check this side first. We'll ride one mile west from here, then one mile east. If necessary, we'll repeat that on the other side.'

When the search along the north bank produced a negative result, they crossed to the south bank, and rode along it to the west, with Josh in the lead. They had covered about a mile, and Josh was just about ready to turn back, when his eye was caught by some faint marks on the ground. He dismounted and followed the marks to a point thirty yards from the bank. Here he stopped, closely examined the ground, then called to Dan to join him. He pointed down to the horse tracks he had found.

'These are the tracks of Morgan and the others,' he said. 'They did their best to wipe them out between here and the bank. Looks like they're heading west, probably on the way to another hiding-place. Let's see if we can follow them there.'

They followed the tracks until it was too dark for Josh to see them, then rested till daybreak, when they resumed the chase. Josh told Dan that one of the horses they were following appeared to have gone lame, and soon after they left camp they noticed that the tracks were now leading in a south-westerly direction. As they rode on, they could see, ahead of them, a large ominous black area of cloud which was moving slowly in their direction, and growing more threatening by the minute.

'Just what we don't want,' said Josh. 'Looks like we're due for a drenching. And there's heavy rain now, ahead of us. It's liable to wash out the tracks we're aiming to follow.'

It was not long before they found themselves subjected to a heavy and lengthy downpour of rain which quickly obliterated the tracks which they were following. They rode on in the same direction and it was still raining heavily when they came in sight of a swing station on a stagecoach route. It consisted of little more than a house, granary, stable and small corral. Here, the stagecoach horses were changed, and a quick snack was given to passengers.

As they rode up to the door, it opened and a twelve-year-old boy came out and stood facing them. His eyes were swollen and his face was strained. He was Johnny Farren, son of the man who was in charge of the swing station. He had been watching their approach through the window and, on seeing the lawman's badge on Dan's vest he had laid down the shotgun he was holding and had gone out to meet them. Looking at the boy's face, Dan and Josh sensed that he was badly shocked and in some kind of trouble. They both dismounted, and followed Johnny inside.

'You all right, boy?' asked Dan.

Haltingly, and obviously deeply distressed, Johnny told of how, on the previous day, four men had ridden up to the swing station with a lame horse. He had been working in the stable when he heard a shot outside. Looking through a window he had seen his father lying motionless on the ground. One of the men started walking towards the stable and Johnny had hidden under a pile of straw. The man had taken his father's saddle horse and the four men men had then departed.

'My pa was dead,' said the boy. 'Shot through the

head. I pulled him in the stable and covered him with a sheet. I've been waiting for the northbound coach to get here. My name's Johnny Farren. What are you doing here?'

'We're after the men who killed your father,' said Dan. 'Was one of them riding a pinto?'

'Yes,' said Johnny. 'That was the lame horse that they left behind.

Dan took a look at the boy's father and the lame pinto which Johnny had put in the corral. He was sure it was Morgan's mount.

When the stagecoach arrived, Dan told the driver what had happened and showed him the body of Johnny's father. Torrential rain was still falling outside.

'There's a home station twenty-four miles ahead,' said the driver. 'I'll get them to send somebody back here to run this station for the time being. And my passengers can wait for food and drink till we get to the next swing station. I guess you'll be going after the men who did this?'

'Trouble is,' said Josh, 'we've got no idea which direction the gang was heading when they left here. And this rain has washed out all the tracks for miles around.'

'I guess you're right,' said the driver. 'I reckon this rainstorm is pretty widespread. We've been travelling through it the last two hours or so.

'What about the boy?' he went on. 'We could take him with us to the next home station.'

'Let's see what he says,' Dan suggested, and they went back into the house. Dan told Johnny that somebody would be coming back from the next home station to take charge. He asked him if he had any kinfolk near by. Johnny said that he knew of only one relative and that was a sister of his mother, who was married to a man working a homestead somewhere near a town called Tremona. Since his mother's death a year ago, they had not heard from her.

Dan took Josh aside. 'After all that rain,' he said, 'I reckon we've lost the Morgan gang for now. The main thing was to rescue Jamie, and you're mainly responsible for us doing that. I still aim to carry on looking for the gang, but I reckon you've done your bit. Go back to Amarillo. As for myself, I have a hankering to see Ruth. So my idea is that we stay here till the new man turns up to run the place, then I'll take Johnny to his folks near Tremona, if that's what he wants. And you can head north for Amarillo. What d'you think?'

'I've got to say,' said Josh, 'that every now and then, 'specially when I'm lying on a bedroll on the hard ground on a cold wet night, with more than a touch of the rheumatics, I realize I'm getting too old for this kind of life. That soft bed I have in Amarillo is mighty inviting. So if that's the way you want it that's what we'll do. But are you aiming to quit the Texas Rangers?'

'I don't know yet,' said Dan, 'but whatever

happens, I'm still set on catching up with Morgan and the others as soon as I get some idea where to look. Let's go and see what Johnny wants to do.'

They found him outside, helping the driver change the horses which had been pulling the stage-coach.

'The boy's got grit,' observed Josh as they waited until the work was completed. Then Dan spoke to the youngster and asked him if he would like to accompany him to Tremona to join his aunt and uncle. Near to tears, Johnny nodded his head.

Dan told the driver that he would take the boy to his folks near Tremona and said he and Josh would stay at the swing station until help arrived. Meantime they would bury the body. He gave the driver some money and asked him to arrange for a suitable saddle horse for the boy to be brought to the swing station.

When the stagecoach had departed, Dan dug a grave for the dead man next to that of his wife and he and Josh, with the boy, stood over it while Dan said a few words.

Early in the evening two men arrived to take over the running of the swing station. The one in charge was called Tanner. They were leading a horse. Tanner handed some money back to Dan.

'This horse for the boy is supplied by the company,' he said. 'And his father had some money coming. It's in this envelope.'

He handed the money to Johnny, then passed on

to Dan the thanks of the company for taking the boy to his kinfolk.

Early the following morning Josh left for Amarillo and Dan and Johnny headed for Tremona.

EIGHT

It was late afternoon when Dan and Johnny rode into Tremona and headed for the livery stable. Ruth, helping her father inside the stable, saw them through the open door. Calling to her father, she ran outside and smiled up at them, wondering who the boy could be. Her father joined her as the two riders dismounted.

'Dan,' said Ruth. 'It's good to see you back. We've been wondering how you and Josh were doing. Is he all right?'

'Josh is fine,' said Dan, 'and I'm glad to *be* back. 'I've a lot to tell you. But before that, Johnny here is aiming to join up with his aunt and uncle. They work a homestead somewhere near here. Their name is Darwell.'

'Ruth and me, we knew the Darwells pretty well,' said the liveryman. 'But they sold their homestead about three months ago. Reckoned they could make a better living in California. Said they would have a good look round there before settling down again. We haven't heard from them since they left, and as far as I know, nobody else around here has.'

Dan put his arm around the boy's shoulders. 'Well, Johnny,' he said. 'It looks like you're stuck with me for a while, until we can find out where your folks have settled.'

Looking at Johnny's face, Ruth and her father could sense the distress he was feeling over the sudden loss of his father and the uncertain future which lay ahead of him.

'It just so happens,' said the liveryman, 'that I badly need somebody to help out in the stable here. I was wondering if Johnny would do that for the time being.'

Johnny looked up at him. 'All right,' he said. 'I know all about horses.'

'That's settled then,' said Ruth. 'You two can have the spare bedroom.'

After the horses had been tended to they all went inside, where Dan told Ruth and her father what had happened since he and Josh left Tremona.

'I've got no notion,' he concluded, 'of where Morgan and the others are right now. But I'm going to telegraph Texas Ranger Captain Armstrong at Fort Worth to let me know of any reports of Morgan or any of the men with him being sighted. So if it's all right with you I'll stay on here for the time being. Johnny's going to help you with the horses, but maybe there are some other jobs I can help you with as well?'

'You're welcome to stay on with me and Ruth,' said the liveryman, 'and there's some repair jobs I've been putting off for far too long. I'd be obliged if you'd get started on them.'

'I guess I can help out with that,' said Dan. 'I was brought up on a cattle ranch.'

The next morning Dan sent a telegraph message to Captain Armstrong.

Then he made enquiries round town and at the homestead which had been owned by Johnny's uncle. But nobody had heard from them since their departure, although they had promised to let the new owner of the homestead know their whereabouts when they finally settled. Dan returned to the livery stable and gave Johnny the news.

'You know, Johnny,' he said, 'that you're welcome to stay here till news comes through from your folks. And when it does, I'll make sure you get out to them as quick as we can fix it.'

Dan started on the repair work in and outside the stable, and Johnny settled down to the job of helping the liveryman with the horses.

Following the killing of Johnny's father at the swing station, Morgan and the others rode to a hideout in a small secluded canyon sixty miles to the south. After a week had passed, Morgan, who had shaved off his beard to alter his appearance, rode back alone to the swing station. As he rode up to it, Tanner and his assistant came out of the stable and stood looking at him. Morgan stopped in front of them. With considerable effort he conjured up the faint semblance of a smile on his hard, ruthless face.

'Howdy,' he said. 'I have a thirsty horse here. Was hoping you might help out.'

Tanner motioned to a nearby water trough. 'Help yourself,' he said, and accompanied Morgan as he led his horse to the water. As the animal drank, the outlaw spoke to Tanner.

'I passed through here on a stagecoach a short while back,' he said. 'I had a talk with the stock tender. What's happened to him?'

'You ain't heard, then?' said Tanner, always glad of the chance of a talk with the occasional passing stranger. 'A week ago Morgan and his gang was here. Farren was in charge of the station. They shot him dead, took one of our horses, and left a lame one behind. His young boy saw it all.'

'It's all wrong,' said Morgan, 'the way these outlaws can roam around, raising hell, and the law don't seem to be able to do anything about it. What happened to the boy?'

'He hid from the gang,' said Tanner. 'And soon after, when I took over, he rode off with a Texas Ranger called Kennedy, who'd been trailing the gang. Kennedy was taking Johnny to his aunt and uncle on a homestead near Tremona. A man who'd been helping him rode off to the north.'

'Let's hope the boy settles down there,' said Morgan. 'That must be a big shock for a young boy, seeing his father shot dead like that.'

Morgan left the swing station shortly after and rode back to the hideout. He told the others what he had learnt.

'We'll ride south tomorrow,' he said, 'and find a hideout near Tremona. That hollow east of town, where we stayed once before in that old abandoned shack, would suit us fine. It's well away from all the trails in the area. Like I told you, our first job will be to find Kennedy and kill him. Maybe he'll still be in the area. If not, maybe we can pick up his trail from there.'

When they reached the hollow, they found it deserted, with no sign that it had been occupied recently. Morgan decided to stay there while they found out whether Kennedy was still in the area. But it would be too risky for any one of them to ride into town to make enquiries. Morgan called Jackson over. He was the youngest member of the gang. Tall and gangling, with a fresh cheerful face which belied his vicious brutal nature, he was the least likely member of the gang to draw attention to himself.

'Find a homestead near to Tremona,' Morgan told him, 'and see if you can find out where Kennedy is right now. And do it without giving any hint that you're looking for him yourself.'

Jackson rode off towards Tremona. About twelve miles away from the town he spotted the buildings of a homestead and headed towards them. As he drew near, Garrett, the homesteader, came out of the barn. Jackson rode up to him.

'Howdy,' he said, smiling down at the home-steader. 'I've been and got myself lost. Was aiming to call at Tremona. I guess it must be somewhere around here. I'd be obliged if you'd point me in the right direction.'

'Ride due west for twelve miles and you can't miss it,' said Garrett.

'Thanks,' said Jackson. 'It's a while since I was there. It sure is a quiet peaceful sort of town.'

'Not *that* quiet and peaceful,' said Garrett. 'We've only been here a short while, but we heard that not long before we came the Morgan gang had been found hiding out near by. And then, after we'd taken over this homestead, a Texas Ranger called Kennedy turned up in town with a young boy whose father had been killed by the Morgan gang at a swing station up north. The boy was related to the folks who sold us this homestead.'

'That's pretty hard on a youngster, losing his pa like that,' said Jackson. 'Has he gone to join his kinfolk?'

'Right now, nobody here knows where they are,' said Garrett. 'He and the Ranger are staying in town with Dennison the liveryman and his daughter. The talk in town yesterday was that Kennedy and Ruth Dennison are mighty friendly. Seems the Ranger is taking some leave. He's helping the liveryman with some repairs at the stable.'

Pleased at the ease with which the information he

required had been obtained from the homesteader, Jackson chatted for a short while on other topics before leaving. He rode to the west until he was out of sight of the homestead buildings, then circled round and returned to the hideout. He told Morgan and the others what he had found out.

'That's good news,' said Morgan. 'It looks like Kennedy's a sitting duck. We'll finish him off quick, then we can start planning our next operation. Kennedy won't be expecting any trouble, so I reckon two men riding into town after dark should be enough for the job.'

He pointed to Jackson, then Perry, a short stocky man with sandy hair and a scarred ugly face.

'You two will go,' he said. 'Aim to ride into town soon after dark. Try and catch them all together at supper. Kill Kennedy and tie the others up to give you time to get away before the alarm is raised. When you get back here we'll all move on.'

When Perry and Jackson reached Tremona after dark they rode slowly along the deserted street until they spotted the livery stable. Light was showing from inside. They carried on past the stable, then, further along the street they turned and rode between two buildings and approached the stable from the rear. Well back from the building they dismounted and tied their horses to a post. Looking through the darkness towards the rear of the stable and the adjacent house, they could see a light showing through a window at the rear of the house.

As they watched, a door at the back of the stable opened and two men and a boy came out, leaving a lighted lamp inside. Half a minute later a door at the rear of the house opened and the two men and a boy went inside.

'We're in luck,' said Jackson. 'That could be Kennedy and the liveryman, with the boy, going in for supper. Let's go take a look.'

They approached the rear of the house, and went up to the window of the living room. There was a small gap between the curtains, and Jackson, holding his pistol, looked through it. He had a partial view of the table at which meals were taken. He could see, seated at the table, the boy and the liveryman. Then a young woman joined them. But there was no sign of Kennedy. Perhaps, thought the outlaw, his quarry was seated at the table out of his sight.

But then he saw Kennedy, unarmed, walking up to the others. He raised his pistol, but before he could take proper aim his target had sat down at the table, out of sight. He cursed inwardly, and motioned to Perry to join him as he moved away from the window.

'They're all sitting at the table,' he said, 'but I can't get a clear shot at Kennedy through the window. We'll have to go inside.'

Jackson and his companion walked up to the rear door of the house which led directly into the living room. Gently, Jackson tried to open it, but it was fastened on the inside. The two outlaws looked for something with which they could ram the door and so achieve a sudden entry, totally unexpected by the people inside. They found a pile of stout fence posts lying on the ground. They selected the heaviest they could find and carried it to a point from which, carrying the post, they could take a straight run at the door.

Inside the house, just as the two outlaws found a suitable battering ram, Dan rose from the table and went up to the room he was sharing with Johnny. Ruth had asked him if she could see a small framed photograph, which Dan carried with him, of his parents on the Rocking K Ranch. He found the photograph and left the room. Walking towards the head of the stairs, he stopped short as he heard the sound of the door bursting open under the impact of the ram. He slipped the photograph into his pocket and ran back to the room for his Colt Peacemaker, then returned to the top of the stairs.

When the door burst open, the two outlaws dropped the ram and drew their pistols as they rushed into the room. Jackson was in the lead. The three people seated at the table half-rose to their feet, then sat down again as they saw the guns in the outlaws' hands. Immediately, Jackson realized that Dan was missing.

'Cover the ones at the table,' he told Perry, in a voice audible to Dennison and the others. 'If anybody moves or makes a sound, kill them.'

Quickly, he checked that Dan was nowhere on the ground floor. Then he stood against the wall close to the foot of the stairs, out of sight of Dan above.

Standing at the top of the stairs, Dan could only guess at what had happened below. He thought he had heard a strange voice, and now there was a complete unnatural silence. He was sure that there were intruders below, probably holding his friends at the table at gunpoint. With his cocked Peacemaker in his hand, he moved down the stairs a couple of steps, then halted. From this point the table was not in view and he could see none of the occupants of the room below.

He took the framed photograph of his parents from his pocket and threw it down the stairs. It skidded over the bare timber top of the third step up, then dropped on to the one below. In the dead silence, the resulting sounds were clearly audible to everyone in the room. Jackson raised his pistol and leaned sideways to shoot the man he believed to be nearing the bottom of the stairs. Ruth jumped up, screaming a warning to Dan, and ran towards Jackson. She was halfway there when a bullet from Perry's six-gun struck her in the chest. She faltered, then sank to the floor.

Dan, standing more than halfway up the stairs, saw Jackson's gun and head appear in view, and before the outlaw had realized just where his opponent was standing, Dan shot him through the head.

The wound was fatal. Seeing his partner fall, Perry lost his nerve. He bolted through the door as a hurried shot from Dan sent a bullet into his left shoulder. He ran to his horse and rode fast out of town. Dan started to follow him, then saw Ruth lying on the floor, with Dennison and Johnny, both shocked by the gunfire, standing by the table. He ran up to her and knelt by her side. He was joined by her father. They could see the bullet hole in her dress. She was still breathing, but unconscious. The liveryman rose to his feet. 'This looks bad,' he said. 'I'll go get Doc Emery.'

Dan carried Ruth up to her bedroom, then dragged the body of Jackson outside.

'Is Miss Ruth going to be all right?' asked Johnny, still badly shaken by recent events.

'I sure do hope so, Johnny,' said Dan, himself desperately worried about her condition. 'Let's see what the doctor can do.'

He went back to the bedroom and was shortly joined by Doc Emery and Ruth's father. Emery examined her while the others stood anxiously by. Gently, the doctor probed to establish the exact location of the bullet. When he had finished he straightened up and spoke to the two men watching him. He looked concerned.

'I can feel the bullet,' he said, 'but it's mighty close to the heart. I don't have the skill or experience to extract it safely. I'm scared I might damage the heart.'

'Do you know anybody with that skill and experience?' asked Dan.

'Only one man that I know of,' Emery replied, 'and that's an ex-Army surgeon called Edison. He lives in Fort Worth now. I went to a talk of his only a couple of weeks ago.'

'I'm going to set off for Fort Worth right now,' said Dan, 'and see if I can get Edison to come here.'

'All right,' said the doctor. 'I think Ruth may come round soon, but she'll have to stay quiet in bed till that bullet comes out. Give me a pen and paper and I'll write a letter to Edison. It'll be ready in a few minutes.'

'I'll go and saddle your horse,' said the liveryman, and left for the stable. Johnny went with him.

Dan went upstairs for the things he needed to take with him. Before leaving the room he took the Wanted poster relating to Jackson and tore it into small pieces. When he went downstairs Emery was just finishing the letter.

When the wounded Perry reached the hideout to report the failure of the mission, Morgan was incensed.

'Are you sure Jackson's dead?' he asked.

'No doubt about it,' Perry replied. 'He was shot in the head. I saw him fall. Now maybe one of you will dig out that bullet in my shoulder.'

The bullet was not deeply embedded, and was fairly easy to remove. The wound was washed and bandaged. Then Morgan spoke.

'This ain't finished yet,' he said, enraged at the loss of one more member of his gang. 'But it's clear we can't say here. We'd best move on.'

NINE

When Dan rode into Fort Worth around noon he made immediate enquiries as to the whereabouts of Edison. He found the doctor in his house near the centre of town. He was a slim, middle-aged man of average height, neatly dressed in black. He listened to Dan's account of the shooting of Ruth, and read the letter from Doc Emery. He looked up at Dan.

'From what I read here,' he said, 'there's a chance that I can help. But I can't guarantee anything. I have several patients to see today, but I could catch the southbound stage to Tremona in the morning.'

'I'm mighty obliged,' said Dan. 'I'll head back myself later today and meet you when the stage rolls in.'

Dan left the doctor's house and went to the office of Ranger Captain Armstrong. He told him about the shooting of Ruth and the death of Jackson. He said that he thought the man with Jackson was Perry, who had escaped, possibly wounded.

'I'm sorry about your friend getting shot,' said Armstrong, 'and let's hope she pulls round. Edison is a good doctor. So Morgan only has two men with him now. Are you figuring to go after them?'

'That can wait,' said Dan. 'What I'm worried about right now is Ruth. We're aiming to get married. Doc Emery told me that bullet could kill her if it ain't taken out soon by a competent surgeon. I'm hoping Edison will be able to do that.'

Dan rested for a few hours and had a meal. Then he left for Tremona. On his arrival there he called at the doctor's house to tell him that Doctor Edison would be arriving on the noon stage. Emery told him that Ruth was now conscious, and was lying on her bed with instructions to move as little as possible. Dan went on to the livery stable and went up to see Ruth. Her father was with her. She was pale and weak from shock and loss of blood, but managed a smile as she saw Dan come in. He sat on the bed and held her hand as he told her and her father that Edison was on his way there. The liveryman left, and Dan stayed with Ruth until just before noon, when he went to await the arrival of the stagecoach. He was joined by Emery.

The stage arrived on time and Edison was taken to the liveryman's house. He carefully examined Ruth; then, with Emery assisting, he embarked on the delicate task of extracting the bullet without endangering the life of his patient. Deeply worried, Dan and Dennison waited downstairs with Johnny, who had become attached to Ruth since his arrival in Tremona.

After a lengthy interval, Doctor Edison came downstairs. He told them that the bullet had been extracted. He said that Ruth was out of danger and he expected a full recovery, in the care of Doctor Emery, over the next few weeks. He himself, he said, would be returning to Fort Worth by the next stagecoach. They thanked him for his help and paid his fee. He headed for the hotel.

Over the following days Ruth's condition steadily improved. Dan divided his time between sitting with and tending to her, and carrying on with the repairs around the stable. A week after the shooting he and Ruth were in the bedroom, with Ruth sitting up in the bed, discussing their future.

'I'm mighty sorry, Ruth,' said Dan, 'that I brought this trouble on you and your father. I don't know how Morgan got to find out that I was here. It seems clear now that he's dead set on killing me in revenge for the loss of his men. So I've got to carry on with the job I started after Jamie was kidnapped. I've got no option but to do my best to put what's left of the Morgan gang out of circulation for good.'

'Father and I don't blame you for what's happened to me,' said Ruth, 'and I understand that you must finish the job you set out to do. But it scares me to think about you facing up to those villains alone. I. . . .'

She broke off as they heard someone coming

upstairs. A moment later, her father appeared in the doorway. Another man was behind him.

'You have a visitor,' said the liveryman, and stood aside to reveal Josh Brennan, the man who had helped to rescue Jamie.

'Josh!' shouted Dan. 'What in blazes are *you* doing here?'

'I heard about Ruth getting shot,' said Josh, 'and I sure am glad to find that she's well on the mend. I know what an obstinate cuss you can be, Dan. I knew you'd be aiming to finish the job we started on, and I figured you could do with some help. Like you, I know I can't rest easy till the job is finished. When that happens maybe I'll be content to settle down and enjoy that comfortable bed of mine and sit out on my porch, smoking my pipe, and looking back on days long gone.'

Ruth smiled at him. 'I feel a whole lot better for seeing you, Josh,' she said. 'I've been worrying about Dan going after those villains on his own.'

'Don't you worry, Ruth,' said Josh. 'We've only got three to deal with now.'

He went on to tell them that he had travelled down on the stagecoach, and had taken a room at the hotel. Dan told Josh about Johnny's kinfolk having moved West. He also told him that he himself was staying in Tremona at least until Ruth was fully recovered.

'Maybe we'll get some news about the Morgan gang in the meantime,' he said.

'My guess is,' said Josh, 'that Morgan and the others have crossed the Red River into the Indian Territory, especially if one of them is wounded. Whatever happens, I'll be ready to leave here when you are.'

Over the next two weeks, during which Ruth made a full recovery, Josh helped Dan to finish the remaining repair work in and around the stable. The last task had been completed and they were standing with Johnny and the liveryman just inside the stable door.

'I'm real obliged for the repair work,' said Dennison, 'and I couldn't have managed without young Johnny here. He sure knows how to look after horses, and he's been doing a man's job.'

Johnny flushed with pleasure, and they were just about to break up when they saw a short, elderly man, weather-beaten and roughly dressed, appear outside the stable door. He was leading a mule and a burro.

'Howdy folks,' he said. 'Would one of you be Ranger Kennedy?'

'That's me,' said Dan. 'Something I can do for you?'

'I'm Hank Leary,' the old man replied. 'Like you see, I'm a prospector. Started in '49 and been looking for that big bonanza ever since. I ain't never struck it real lucky, and likely I'm a fool to carry on. But I can't quit. It's in my blood. The reason I'm here is because maybe I can help you. I've just been in the saloon for a beer, and I happened to hear about the Morgan gang shooting a woman here a few weeks back. They were saying that the lady was a friend of yours, and that one of the gang was likely wounded. Maybe I can help you to find them.'

'Please come into the house, Mr Leary,' said the liveryman. 'We can talk better in there. Meantime, if you like, Johnny here can tend to the mule and burro.'

Inside the house Leary told Dan and the others how, about three weeks ago, he had been prospecting north of Fort Worth.

'Late in the afternoon I spotted on a hillside the entrance to the tunnel of an old abandoned mine,' he told them. 'Most of the shuttering over the entrance had fallen away and I figured I'd take a look inside with a lamp. The tunnel looked pretty safe, and there was one spot, well back from the entrance, where it widened out considerable. I figured I'd stay there for the night with the mule and burro, and I brought them inside.'

'Later in the evening,' he went on, 'I thought I heard voices. I put out the lamp and felt my way along the tunnel towards the entrance. Then I saw a man walk into the tunnel with a lighted match. I stopped. He lit a few more, but before he got near me I saw him turn round and go back. I waited a short while, then I snuck up to the entrance and stood behind the shuttering that was left. I could see pretty well through a gap in the shuttering. Just outside the tunnel a campfire was burning bright. Two men were sitting by it. One had his shirt and vest off. It looked like he had a shoulder wound that was being tended by a third man kneeling by him.'

'You think you were looking at the Morgan gang?' asked Dan. 'Just give me a minute.'

He ran upstairs and took from a drawer the Wanted notices for the remaining three members of the Morgan gang. He carried them downstairs and showed them to Leary. 'Would these be the men?' he asked.

Leary studied the posters closely before replying.

'I'm sure of it,' he said. 'I got a good look at their faces. And according to the poster, Morgan's first name is Matt. That's what I heard one of the others call him. And that's not all. I could hear most of what they were saying before they settled down for the night.'

'This sounds mighty interesting,' said Dan. 'What did you hear?'

'I'll just give you the interesting bits,' said Leary. 'They were aiming to cross the Red River near Red River Station. Then they were going to ride into the Indian Territory for about twenty miles to stay with a man called Wilson where they could rest up for a while and get a doctor to tend to the shoulder wound. They didn't say where this Wilson was actually living, or anything else about him. So what it boils down to is that all I can really tell you is that the gang were meeting up with a man called Wilson about twenty miles from the Red River. Is that any use to you?'

'It sure is,' said Dan, 'and we're obliged to you for bringing us the information. Josh and I will ride into the Nations to see if we can find this man Wilson. Maybe Morgan and the others are still there.'

The liveryman invited Leary to stay for supper, but he declined the offer. Shortly after, he rode out of town, still supremely confident that his luck was about to change.

Soon after Leary's departure Ruth came in. She had been visiting a woman friend. Dan told her the news.

'Josh and I will be leaving in the morning,' he said. 'We'll cross the Red River and try to find this man Wilson. We'll call in at Fort Worth to let Captain Armstrong know what we're doing. He'll pass the information on to the US marshal at Fort Smith. If we get the chance we'll call in some help from the law.'

'You know that I'm going to be worried,' said Ruth. 'But I understand that it's something you have to do.'

Early the following morning Dan and Josh rode off to the north.

TEN

When Dan and Josh reached Fort Worth they went to see Captain Armstrong. They told him about the information they had received from Leary and their intention to ride into the Indian Territory. They asked him if he knew of anyone called Wilson living in the area north of, and around twenty miles from, the Red River.

'Can't think of any criminal of that name who might be there,' said Armstrong, 'and since it's outside our jurisdiction, I'm not familiar with the area. I'm sorry I can't help you with that. But I'll let Fort Smith know that you're in the territory.'

Dan and Josh rode on from Fort Worth and crossed the Red River a little way west of Red River Station in the late afternoon. They rode on in a northerly direction until darkness fell, then looked around for a suitable campsite. As they were doing this, Dan noticed, a little way ahead of them, a flickering light which could be coming from a campfire.

He pointed it out to Josh.

'It's unlikely,' said Dan, 'but I suppose it's just possible that Morgan and the others are camped there. We'd better sneak up and take a look.'

They rode towards the light, then secured their horses when they were still a short distance away from the fire. They advanced on foot until they were able to look at it from behind a small patch of brush. They could see six men seated by it, taking some food and drink. They were not close enough to be able to identify any of the men.

'It don't look like the Morgan gang,' said Josh, 'unless he's picked up some more men. I'd better move up to that boulder close to the fire. I can get a good look at them from there and maybe I'll be able to hear what they're saying.'

'All right,' said Dan, knowing that Josh was much more capable than himself of reaching the boulder without being spotted. 'I'll stay here and give you a hand if you get into trouble.'

Josh melted into the darkness and Dan continued to watch the men at the fire. They appeared to start a discussion, in voices only faintly audible to Dan, which continued for the next twenty minutes or so, before it ended.

Peering around the boulder, Josh could see that none of the members of the Morgan gang was present. However, he recognized one of the men and listened to the discussion with considerable interest. When it was over, he was just preparing to return to

Dan when one of the men suddenly rose and walked towards the boulder, and a little way past it, before stopping. Josh had no time to move away without being seen. Dressed in dark clothing, he flattened himself against the boulder, and took out his six-gun, prepared to shoot or pistol-whip the man if this became necessary. The man turned half a minute later and walked towards the fire, which was burning brightly. Partly blinded by the flames, he failed to see Josh and sat down again by the fire.

Josh stayed where he was a little longer, but when indications were that the men were about to turn in after a long day's ride, he returned to Dan.

'What I heard there was mighty interesting,' he said. 'That's a gang of rustlers over there. They were actually talking over their plan to steal a trail herd belonging to a Bar 10 ranch. The herd is heading for Dodge City over the Chisholm Trail. It's expected to cross the Red River tomorrow morning, and they plan to take it over tomorrow night. They'll move in when the trail boss and all the hands, except the two guarding the cattle overnight, are asleep. They didn't say where they were aiming to take the herd after that.'

'It's clear then,' said Dan, 'that we'll have to post-pone our search for Morgan. We need to warn the trail boss and help him fight off the rustlers.'

'You're right,' said Josh. 'And there's one other thing. I recognized the leader of the gang over there. Before you joined the Rangers in Amarillo he was brought to trial there for beating up a saloon girl so bad she near died. He was sent to prison for a spell. Before that he'd been under suspicion of being leader of a gang of rustlers who had no qualms about leaving the trail boss and all the trail hands dead. But there wasn't enough evidence to bring him to trial. His name's Portman.'

'We'd better ride back to the Red River and camp there until the herd crosses over in the morning,' said Dan. 'Then we can tell the trail boss about the rustlers who are aiming to take over his herd.'

It was still dark when Dan and Josh reached the north bank of the Red River opposite Red River Station. They rested there until dawn, then watched out for the Bar 10 trail herd. It was an hour before they saw a herd approaching the far bank. The river was low at the time and the crossing was made without incident. When it was completed the herd, guided by the trail hands, moved off towards the north. Ten miles or so on, they would be bedded down for the night.

Dan and Josh rode towards Cartwright, the trail boss, whom they had seen giving orders to the hands. He was riding by the chuck wagon, talking to the cook who was driving it. The trail boss was a tall, slim man in his early fifties, competent looking, with a weather-beaten face and some years' experience as a trail boss behind him. He and the cook looked curiously at the two riders as they approached.

'Well I'm darned,' said the cook. 'The rider on the

left is a Texas Ranger. When I was cook on the Diamond B in the Panhandle, he called in once to ask if anybody had seen a stagecoach robber he was chasing. I seem to recollect his name was Brennan. What in blazes is he doing in the Nations?'

When Dan and Josh reached Cartwright, he stopped to speak to them. The chuck wagon moved on.

'Howdy,' said Dan, taking his Ranger badge from his pocket and showing it to the trail boss. 'I'm Dan Kennedy, and this is my partner Josh Brennan. Is this herd from the Bar 10 ranch?'

'I'm Cartwright,' sad the trail boss. 'This is a Bar 10 trail herd, but I'm wondering what a couple of Texas Rangers are doing in the Nations.'

Briefly, Dan told the trail boss what had brought him and Josh into the Indian Territory. Then he gave him details of the chance encounter with the rustlers, during which they had learnt of the gang's plan to steal the Bar 10 herd.

'This is real bad news,' said Cartwright. 'I ain't lost a trail herd yet, but I know the risk is always there. We carry some six-guns and rifles, but the seven hands with me, including the cook, ain't exactly gunfighters. They're no match for the rustlers.'

'We aim to help you deal with them,' said Dan. 'There's no time to get any deputy US marshals here. When they strike tonight we need to be ready for them. We know their plan is to avoid a stampede if possible. They figure to move in on the camp first, and to kill all the sleeping men. If the herd is well away from the camp they'll do this by shooting them. Then they aim to deal with the two men guarding the herd. We need to work on a plan that has the best chance of keeping us all alive. And we've got to be mighty careful about choosing the location of tonight's bed ground.

'I was aiming to ride on ahead right now to choose a stopping place for tonight,' said the trail boss. 'I've got a good idea now of what we need. You can ride along with me.'

They rode up to the chuck wagon, where Cartwright had a few words with the cook. Then they rode on fast to the north, leaving the herd behind them. Eight miles on, they started looking for a suitable bed ground, after agreeing what was required. A mile further on they came to a small area of flat ground, a little way off the trail, circled by large clumps of brush.

'This is just right for the camp,' said the trail boss, and Dan agreed.

'Now let's find a bed ground for the cattle,' he said.

They settled on a shallow basin, not too close to the camp. It was large enough to accommodate the herd. Then Cartwright rode back to the head of the approaching herd. Dan and Josh stayed behind, cutting down some of the brush at the campsite and piling it on the ground.

When the herd arrived it was driven into the basin.

108

Then the trail boss called the men together. After introducing Dan and Josh, he told them about the intention of a gang of rustlers to steal the herd during the night. He explained the plan which had been decided on to thwart the gang. He said that the two men guarding the herd in the basin when the rustlers arrived would be armed, but should ignore the sound of gunfire at the camp.

'We're hoping,' he said, 'that the rustlers will never get as far as the herd.'

After supper, six bedrolls were laid down in positions near the fire. A tied bundle of brush was placed on top of each one and this was covered by a blanket, to give a passable impression, in the darkness, of a sleeping man. Arms and ammunition were handed out to all the hands. An hour before midnight, the two hands guarding the cattle were relieved. Then Dan, with Cartwright and the hands, took up positions in the patches of brush overlooking the fire, where they could hide from the rustlers. Josh left on foot to circle the campfire at a distance, watching out for the arrival of the gang.

An hour after midnight Josh ran into the camp, to tell Dan and the others that he had heard the gang approaching and they would arrive shortly. He threw some more wood on the fire, then joined the others.

It was ten minutes before the six rustlers were seen as they approached the fire, moving slowly and silently, and holding their six-guns. Each of them crept up to one of the bedrolls and stood over it, his pistol pointing downwards. At a shouted signal from Portman, they all fired bullets into the bundles of brush underneath the blankets.

Immediately, they came under fire from the men hidden in the brush who, with no qualms about what they were doing, could see the outlines of the rustlers against the glow from the campfire. The outcome was quick and lethal. Under the hail of gunfire all the rustlers went down, some without firing a shot in retaliation. The firing stopped and Dan and the others left the brush, still holding their weapons, and cautiously approached the men lying on the ground. They found four already dead. The other two, fatally wounded, died within the next ten minutes.

The trail boss sent a hand to tell the night guards with the herd what had happened. Then he spoke to Dan and Josh.

'Thanks to you two,' he said, we came out of that pretty well. Not one of us took a hit. What do we do with these bodies?'

'Josh and I will search them for any identification they might have on them,' said Dan. 'Then they can be buried here.'

The search of the dead men's clothing produced nothing of note. But when their horses were found and brought into camp, one item found in a saddle-bag was of considerable interest to Dan and Josh. It was a crumpled sheet of paper bearing a handwritten message, which read: *Herd expected cross Red on 29th if all goes well. Expect see you in Comanche Wells after, oper-*

110

ation completed. Wilson.

'It seems likely,' said Dan, 'that the Wilson who sent this is the man we're looking for. It's clear he's been helping Portman in his plan to steal the Bar 10 herd. So he *could* know Morgan. This place Comanche Wells, d'you know where it is, Josh?'

'No, I don't,' Josh replied. 'Maybe the trail boss can help.'

Dan showed Cartwright the letter and he told them that Comanche Wells was about thirty miles west, not far north of the Red River.

'I passed through it once,' he said, 'when I was riding back to Texas after a trail drive. I was pressed for time and I just called in at the store for some supplies. There weren't much else there but a two-storey saloon and a livery stable.'

Early the following morning, Dan and Josh took their leave of Cartwright and the trail crew, and headed towards Comanche Wells. Dan's Texas Ranger badge was hidden in his pocket. A little before noon they stopped as they came in sight of the small settlement of Comanche Wells. They could see three large buildings, presumably the saloon, store and livery stable mentioned by Cartwright. In addition there was a small shack, well away from the other buildings. Through his field glasses, Dan could see a man moving around outside the shack.

'It's just possible,' said Dan, 'that Morgan and the others are still there. Before we go near the main buildings, let's have a few words with that man at the shack. Maybe he can give us some useful information.'

They rode towards the shack. As they reached it they saw Henry Nelson, a man in his early seventies, frail and bearded, staggering under the weight of the door he was carrying. As he stepped up on to the boarded floor of the porch outside his front door he stumbled and fell backwards, with the door on top of him. Quickly, Dan and Josh dismounted and ran to help the old man, who was badly shaken by the fall. They lifted the door off him and helped him to a chair standing on the porch.

'I'm obliged to you folks,' said Nelson. 'Trouble is, I ain't as spry as I used to be. I took that door off to repair it, and I was just fixing to put it back when you turned up.'

'We'll fix the door for you,' offered Dan, 'and when we're done, maybe you could tell us something about the history of Comanche Wells.'

'It's a deal,' said Nelson. 'I guess I twisted my ankle. I'll have to rest it for a spell.'

When they had fixed the door back in position, Dan and Josh stood on the porch and listened to Nelson. He told them that the first building there was a store which he himself had opened a long time back, with a Mexican man helping him. There was enough business from folks passing by to make a reasonable profit.

'Then, a couple of years ago,' he went on, 'I was a mite surprised when a man called Wilson turned up and built the saloon and the livery stable. I couldn't figure out how he reckoned to pull in enough business to make a profit. When the work was finished he offered to buy me out. It was a pretty good offer and I was beginning to feel my age. So I accepted it. I didn't have no kinfolk to go to, so I built me this shack and settled down here. And I guess this is where I'll end my days.'

'You've got no friends around to give you a hand when you need it?' asked Dan.

'Nobody,' Nelson replied. 'Everybody else around here works for Wilson, and *he* ain't exactly friendly. I don't know why, but I've got a feeling he don't like having me around.'

'Wilson still being here after two years,' said Dan, 'makes it look like his businesses here are doing well.'

'I can't figure it out,' said Nelson. 'There ain't that many people passing through. But I have a notion that now and then Wilson has people riding in after dark and staying in some rooms at the saloon. I don't go in there myself. Was never one for drinking and gambling.'

'Maybe you'd be better off in a small town south of the Red River in Texas,' suggested Josh. 'Somewhere where you could make a few friends?'

'I'm a mite old to move now,' said Nelson, 'but I'm going to think hard on what you just said.'

'We'll be moving on now, then,' said Dan. 'We don't aim to stay here overnight. Are you going to be all right with that twisted ankle?'

Nelson stood up to test it, then sat down again. 'I reckon it'll be better by morning,' he said. 'I'm mighty obliged to you for fixing that door for me.'

When Dan and Josh left the old man there were stil a couple of hours to go before dark. They rode slowly towards a low ridge to the north, discussing their next move.

'From what Nelson told us,' said Dan, 'it looks like Wilson could be harbouring criminals. Maybe Morgan and his men are still there. I think our best plan is to ride into Comanche Wells after dark and see if we can spot them without being seen ourselves. We'll hide out somewhere on that ridge ahead till after nightfall.'

Josh agreed and as they rode on towards the ridge they spotted a rider approaching from the east on a path which would cross their own.

'Let's see who that is,' said Dan, and they adjusted their pace so that they would intercept the rider. He stopped as they rode up to him, and turned to face them. He was a big man in his early forties. He wore a deputy US marshal badge. Closely, he studied the face of Dan, then Josh.

'Howdy,' said Dan. 'We sure are glad to meet up with you, Deputy.'

He pulled his Texas Ranger badge from his pocket and showed it to the deputy. Then he gave him their names and told him about their pursuit of Morgan and his gang, and their knowledge of Wilson's collusion with Morgan and the rustlers.

'It's possible,' he went on, 'that Morgan is still with Wilson. But this being the Indian Territory, we haven't got the authority to go in and search his place ourselves. We're hoping that you and some other deputies can take that over. We'll help out as much as you like.'

'My name's Truman,' said the deputy. 'That's mighty interesting, what you just told me. I heard about you two chasing the Morgan gang in Texas. I reckon you've turned up enough proof to justify a search of Comanche Wells. I'm on my way now to meet up with three other deputies twenty miles west of here. The operation we were going on can wait. It's clear that the raid on Comanche Wells should come first. There's a chance of picking up other outlaws, apart from Morgan and his gang. I should get back here with my partners around daybreak tomorrow. Where will we find you?'

'We were heading for the top of that ridge,' said Dan. 'We figured to find ourselves a hiding-place up there.'

'Right,' said Truman. 'I'll go with you so we'll know exactly where to find you, when I get back with the others.'

They found a hollow on top of the ridge from which they could see Comanche Wells in the distance. As the deputy left them, heading in a westerly direction, darkness was falling.

'We were lucky meeting up with Truman,' said

Josh. 'Maybe we're getting near the end of our mission.'

They had a meal, then settled down to await the arrival of the deputies the following morning.

ELEVEN

The attack came at ninety minutes past midnight. It was totally unexpected and carried out in complete silence. Josh and Dan were rudely awakened at the same instant by the muzzle of a six-gun jabbed against the side of the head. Ordered not to move, they lay motionless until the campfire had been relit and was burning brightly. Then they were ordered to sit up and their hands were bound. They looked up at the six men who had carried out the attack.

Close to them they recognised Morgan, with Perry and Wright. Standing by those three were two other men they did not recognize. Then a sixth man walked up towards them. It was Truman, the deputy US marshal they had met the previous evening. Shocked, they stared at the deputy, then looked at one another, the realization dawning that Truman must be in cahoots with Morgan and Wilson.

Morgan looked down at the two prisoners. There

117

was a look of grim satisfaction on his bleak ruthless face.

'This is a day I've really been looking forward to,' he said. 'You two have been responsible for the loss of four of my men. Now you're going to pay for that.'

He spoke to one of the two men who were strangers to the prisoners.

'I'm obliged, Wilson, for the help of you and Slater in capturing these two,' he said. 'Me and my men will take charge of them now.'

'I take it you're going to finish them off,' said Wilson, a short thickset man in his early forties. 'They know far too much to stay alive.'

'That's exactly the way I see it myself,' said Truman.

'You can be one hundred per cent sure they're going to end up dead,' said Morgan, 'and their bodies will never be found.'

'I'd like Slater to stay with you to help guard the prisoners till that happens,' said Wilson. 'Then he can report back to me at Comanche Wells.'

'All right,' said Morgan. I'll be glad of an extra hand to help out as long as these two are still alive.'

Shortly after, Wilson and Truman rode off. The prisoners' feet were tied and they were ordered to lie down. Then Perry and Wright guarded them while Morgan and Slater lay down for a brief sleep. Two hours later they changed over with the two guards. During the night Dan and Josh, who were lying close together, had a whispered conversation.

'That Truman sure made fools of us Josh,' said Dan. 'We're in a fine fix now. I wonder how long Morgan reckons to keep us alive? I can't think why he hasn't killed us already.'

'I was wondering that myself,' said Josh. 'I think he means to get rid of us pretty soon. And they're guarding us so close I don't see there's anything we can do about it.'

At daybreak, after everyone including the prisoners had taken breakfast, Morgan spoke to his men and Slater, just out of earshot of Dan and Josh. Dan guessed that they were discussing the fate of their two prisoners. At one point a brief argument seemed to be taking place between Morgan and Slater.

Following the discussion the party headed south towards the Red River. Their hands tied, Josh and Dan were closely guarded by the four men riding with them. They crossed the Red and headed roughly south-west, avoiding all signs of human habitation. Morgan and the others had brought ample supplies with them and the party rode on until dark. The same happened on the following day. During the whole journey, the prisoners were given no indication of the fate in store for them. After supper, lying near the campfire, Dan had a whispered conversation with his partner.

'Do you know where we are, Dan?' asked Josh.

'I've got an idea,' said Dan, 'that we both have the same notion. I think we're pretty close to the Rocking K spread.'

'Exactly what *I* was thinking,' said Josh. 'But why would Morgan want to bring us here?'

'Knowing Morgan like we do,' said Dan, 'the thought just struck me that maybe he's figuring on holding us for ransom. He knows my father is a wealthy man, and I guess he was pretty mad when we rescued young Jamie without any ransom being paid. But there's one thing I'm sure of. He means to kill us whether he gets any ransom money or not. I reckon he's heading for a hideout somewhere around here.'

And Dan proved to be right. After riding on a while after breakfast, they headed for a deep gully, with which Morgan and his men seemed to be familiar, and set up camp there.

In the Rocking K ranch house, on the afternoon of the day on which Morgan and the others set up camp in the gully, Jacob Kennedy and his wife Martha were in the living room. Clint, with his wife Rebecca, and his son Jamie, were away on a short visit to El Paso to see Rebecca's parents. All the ranch hands, apart from the cook and one of the older hands, called Inman, were working out on the range. The cook was in the cookshack, and Inman was working on repairs to the corral fence, some way from the house.

Martha, sitting near a window, was writing a letter to an old friend of hers in San Antonio. She glanced out of the window and noticed a distant rider heading for the house. She glanced out again a little later, and decided that the rider was a stranger.

Then, as he drew closer and she got a good look at his face, she jumped up, stifling a scream, and ran over to her husband, seated at his desk. Startled, he looked up at her.

'Jacob!' she said, urgently, 'there's a man riding up to the house. And I swear it's the outlaw Morgan who kidnapped Jamie. He's alone.'

The rancher jumped to his feet and ran to a cupboard. He took out a double-barrelled shotgun and loaded both barrels. Carrying the weapon, he walked to the door and opened it. Martha was right behind him. Morgan, who had stopped outside the door, was sitting on his mount facing them.

'I'm guessing you're Jacob Kennedy,' said Morgan. 'There's no need for the shotgun. Anything happens to me and your son Dan and his partner Brennan will die. I'm here to parley.'

Kennedy lowered the shotgun and Martha moved to stand by his side.

'Speak your piece,' said the rancher.

'We're holding the two men I just mentioned,' said Morgan. 'They're not far from here. If you want to see them alive again, you'll have to pay me the same ransom I asked for the boy – that's a hundred thousand dollars in used banknotes.'

'You'll get nothing till I have proof that you're holding them prisoner,' said the rancher.

'I can arrange that,' said Morgan. 'You have a line shack due east of here, on the boundary of your range. I saw a hand working on your corral fence as

121

I rode in. I reckon I would recognize him if I saw him again. If he knows the prisoners, I want you to send him to that line shack two days from now. He'll need to arrive there at around four in the afternoon. He won't be harmed, but he'll see your son and his partner alive. Then I'll give him a message for you, telling you when and where to hand over the money. If there's any sign of that hand being followed to the line shack, or if you bring the law into this, the prisoners will both die.'

'I hear what you say,' said the rancher. 'Inman knows my son and his partner. He'll ride to the line shack day after tomorrow.'

'I'll be leaving now,' said Morgan, 'and don't even think of trying to follow me, or having me followed.'

Morgan turned his horse and rode off in the direction from which he had arrived.

Watching him leave, the rancher spoke to his wife. 'I don't think Morgan is lying about holding Dan and Josh,' he said. 'So we'll make a start on getting the money together. But you know, Martha, that even if we give him the money, there's still a chance that he'll kill his two prisoners.'

'I know that,' said Martha, deeply concerned about the situation, 'but they're both very capable men, and we know they'll be alive for three days at least. I'm hoping they'll manage to escape.'

Her thoughts turned to Ruth. Dan had told his parents of their plan to marry as soon as he had dealt with the Morgan gang, and she and her husband had been looking forward to attending the wedding.

'Ruth is probably worried sick about Dan,' she said. 'We've got to let her know what's happening here.'

'You're right,' said her husband. 'I'll get one of the hands to ride to Tremona with a letter for her. We'll ask that she and her father keep the news to themselves. We'll say that we'll let her know of any developments as soon as we can.'

While Martha started to write the letter Kennedy went out to see Inman. He told him what had happened, asking him to keep it secret. Inman, who had known Dan as a young boy, readily agreed to ride out to the line shack at the appointed time and bring the message back. Kennedy then told him to ride on to the range and bring one of the hands, young Jeff Weaver, back to see him as quickly as possible. A few minutes later Inman rode off fast towards the area in which Weaver was working.

Almost two hours passed before the two hands returned. Weaver went to see the rancher.

'I have an important job for you, Jeff,' said Kennedy. 'I've picked you because I reckon that on a good horse you're the fastest rider on my payroll. I have a letter here for the daughter of Dennison, the liveryman in Tremona. I know it's a long ride, but pick out the horse you want and make the best time you can. Take a rest in Tremona before you come back here.

'I'll do the best I can, Mr Kennedy,' said Weaver.

'And I know just the horse I want.'

There were still a couple of hours to go before nightfall when Weaver rode off fast to the east. He rode on through the night and the following day, taking only those periods of rest which were absolutely necessary for himself and his mount. It was late in the evening when he rode up to the livery stable in Tremona. There was no one inside the stable. He knocked on the door of the house. It was opened by Ruth.

'I have a letter for you, miss,' he said. 'I've brung it for you from Mr and Mrs Kennedy on the Rocking K. They said it's urgent.'

He handed the letter to Ruth, who invited him into the living room, where her father was seated. Ruth explained that the stranger had brought her a letter from Dan's parents. Then she opened the letter and read the contents, which ended by saying that the bearer knew nothing of the emergency, and they would prefer that he wasn't told. Watching his daughter, the liveryman, as well as Johnny, saw the look of deep concern on her face as she read the contents of the letter. She read it a second time, then handed it to her father. When he had read it, she pulled herself together, then spoke to Weaver, who was stifling a yawn.

'You look real tuckered out, Mr . . .' she said.

'Jeff Weaver,' he said. 'I feel like I look. I'll find me a bed at the hotel.'

'No need for that,' said Ruth. 'We have a spare bed

you can use after I've whipped up a meal for you. And Johnny here will look after your horse.'

A little later, when Weaver had gone to his bed, followed by Johnny, Ruth spoke to her father.

'I've been thinking, Father,' she said. 'I'm going to the Rocking K. I need to get there just as soon as I can. I can't just sit here waiting for news of Dan. Will you help me?'

Dennison could see that she had made up her mind. He told her that if she took a night stage passing through Tremona in an hour's time, she might be able to get a connection which would take her to Trasco, near the Rocking K. At Trasco, she could hire a horse or buggy to take her to the ranch.

'You get ready,' he said. 'I'll go see the stagecoach agent and get the information we need.'

When he returned he told Ruth that she was booked on the stagecoach, with a connection to Trasco, the whole journey taking about fifteen hours. The stagecoach left Tremona, with Ruth on board, forty minutes later.

On the day following Weaver's departure for Tremona, Clint arrived back at the Rocking K with his wife and Jamie. Jacob and Martha gave them the bad news about the capture of Dan and Josh.

'I can't help thinking,' said Clint, who had taken over the role of foreman of the ranch, 'that we should try and rescue Dan and Josh before Inman sees them at the line shack. Some time after that, I think Morgan means to kill them, considering the way they whittled his gang down. And I think we should tell *all* the hands about what's happened here. They'll keep their mouths shut. And we need their help if we aim to rescue Dan and Josh.'

'I think Clint is right,' said his mother.

'I've been coming round to the same way of thinking myself,' said the rancher. 'Let's go and talk to the hands, Clint. They're all here right now.'

After a brief discussion the two men went out and called the hands together. The rancher explained the dangers of the situation and asked them not to mention it to anyone outside the ranch. Then he handed over to Clint.

'We aim to try and rescue Dan and Josh,' said Clint, 'because we think they'll be killed if we can't manage to free them in time. The first thing we have to do is find out where they're holding the prisoners. We need to do that without the gang knowing they've been located. The place must be somewhere in this area. Then we have to make a rescue attempt. That ain't going to be easy because we've got to get to the prisoners before the gang realizes that we're there. And we're going to need the help of just a few of you, who're willing to volunteer.'

A man in his mid-twenties, called Billy Lightfoot, spoke up. He was a slim, quiet man, wiry and fair-haired. As a young boy, he had been taken by Comanche Indians when his father's small ranch had been raided. His parents had both been killed. He

126

was brought up in the tribe, but had later decided to leave it and enter the world of the white man. An Indian agent had asked Jacob Kennedy if he would take Billy on as a ranch hand, and the rancher had agreed. And Billy had proved to be a capable and tireless worker.

'If you can show me which way Morgan was riding when he left here,' said Billy, 'I will follow his tracks. I will find the place where the gang is hiding, and after it is dark I will find out how many men there are there and how the prisoners are being held. When I have done this I will come back here.'

'You sure you can do this, Billy?' asked Clint.

Billy nodded his head. 'With the Comanche,' he said, 'I have followed the tracks of men and horses many times.'

'All right,' said Clint, and Jacob Kennedy told Billy that when Morgan had left them he had ridden straight from the house to an outcrop visible in the distance, He had passed close to the right side of the outcrop before disappearing from view.

'When Billy gets back,' Clint told the hands, 'we'll get to work on a rescue plan.'

The men dispersed, and ten minutes later Clint and his father watched Billy as he rode off towards the outcrop, taking an occasional look at the ground. When he disappeared from view, the rancher spoke to his son.

'Billy's taken a lot on his shoulders,' he said. 'Let's hope he gets back with the information we need.

Our last chance of rescuing Dan and Josh will be tomorrow night.'

The two men went inside to tell the women what had happened. Then they all resigned themselves to an anxious wait for Billy's return.

TWELVE

Billy Lightfoot returned well before dawn. Clint and his father, resting uneasily in the living room, heard his knock on the door and let him in. Martha also heard the knock, and she came downstairs with Rebecca.

Billy told them that he had located the hideout in a deep gully abut nine miles to the north-west of the line shack, which Inman was to ride to the following day. He had looked down into the gully and had seen two men being held prisoner by four others.

'It looks like Morgan has picked up another man somewhere,' said Clint. 'What happened next, Billy?'

Billy told them that after midnight he climbed down into the gully on foot and got a closer look at the four men, and their prisoners, who appeared to be unhurt. The prisoners were tied hand and foot, and were guarded by two of the men. The other two were sleeping in what looked like an ex-Army tent on the other side of the campfire, which was kept burning. Horses were tied to a picket line a little way up the gully from the fire. In conclusion, Billy gave a detailed description of the gully, with which neither Clint nor his father was familiar. Then he said that he wished to help with the rescue.

'That's a fine job you just did for us, Billy,' said Clint, 'and we're mighty grateful for your offer to help with the rescue. You go and get some sleep. After breakfast we'll work on a plan to rescue Dan and Josh.'

Two hours before noon the hands were called together again, and Clint spoke to them. His father was by his side.

'You've heard what Billy found last night,' he said. 'If we want to get the prisoners out alive we've got to put the two guards out of action without alerting them or the two men in the tent. My father and I will be going, as well as Billy here. We reckon we need three more men with us to do the job. It's not the sort of work you're paid for, and there's no denying it could be dangerous. So we're asking for volunteers. Raise a hand if you're willing to come along.'

Moved by the response, Clint and his father watched as every one of the men standing in front of them held up a hand. Clint selected the three men he considered most suitable for the mission. These three, with Billy, Clint and Jacob went into the ranch house to discuss in detail the forthcoming operation. During this discussion it was decided that they would leave for the gully after dark. And a method of over-

THE LONG HUNT

coming the two guards with the least risk of them shooting the prisoners or raising the alarm, was agreed.

At around four in the afternoon a buggy rolled up to the ranch house just as Jacob Kennedy and his son were about to go inside. Surprised, they saw that the driver was an attractive young woman, a stranger to them. Clint walked up to the buggy and helped her down. The two men could see the look of deep anxiety on her face. She turned and spoke to Jacob.

'I guess this is the Rocking K,' she said, 'and you must be Dan's father. I'm Ruth Dennison. I came as soon as I got your message about Dan and Josh.'

'We've heard a lot about you from Dan,' said Jacob, 'and we're real pleased to meet you. This is Dan's brother Clint. Come inside and meet Martha and Rebecca. We have more news for you about Dan and Josh.'

They went inside and into the living room, where Martha and Rebecca were sitting. Surprised, the two women looked at the stranger.

'This is Ruth, just got here from Tremona,' said the rancher.

Martha rose to her feet and walked over to Ruth. She embraced her, led her to a chair, and introduced Rebecca.

'I had a feeling you might come, Ruth,' she said. 'You must be tired, and real worried about Dan. Has Jacob told you the latest news?'

'I was just going to,' said the rancher, and went on

to tell Ruth about Billy's discovery of the place where Dan and Josh were being held.

'I'm glad you're here, Ruth,' he went on, 'because we've taken a decision here to try and free Dan and Josh, because we think that even if we pay the ransom, they'll be killed. But you have a right to a say in this. What do you think?'

'I agree with you,' said Ruth. 'From what I know of Morgan, he's just plain evil. He would never free Dan and Josh if he had his way.'

'Good,' said the rancher, and he and Clint told her of their plan to rescue the two prisoners during the coming night.

'I'd like to thank Billy for what he did,' said Ruth. 'And the other men who are helping out tonight.'

'All right,' said Clint. 'I know that's something they would appreciate.'

He took Ruth outside and introduced her to the hands. She then thanked Billy and the other three hands Prentice, Mailer and Sully, who would be participating in the rescue attempt. Then she went back into the house to join the women.

The party left after dark, taking two spare saddled horses with them, in case they were needed. As a precaution, it was arranged that the ranch hands remaining behind would guard the ranch house until the others returned. They reached the vicinity of the gully around midnight. Clint sent Billy on ahead to climb down into the gully and confirm that the prisoners were still there under guard as before.

Forty minutes later Billy returned to report that the situation was the same as on the previous evening. The two prisoners, now blindfolded, were lying side by side on the ground, with hands and feet tied. The two armed guards were sitting side by side on the ground, facing the prisoners, occasionally talking to one another.

'Let's go,' said Clint, and leaving the picketed horses behind they all climbed down into the gully, with Billy in the lead. They moved a little way along the bottom of the gully, then stopped well short of the fire, out of sight of the guards.

'Me and Billy go on alone from here,' whispered Clint. 'You come a-running if you hear gunfire. Otherwise, we'll call for you.'

Billy lay down on his belly. Clint did the same. Clint was carrying his Colt .45 Peacemaker with the long barrel. It was a weapon he had learnt to handle with a high degree of proficiency. Billy was carrying an Indian war club, which had been hanging on the wall of the bunkhouse. It had been found by a hand out on the range some years back. It had a wooden handle with a stone head firmly attached, both covered with buckskin.

Billy led the way. Lying flat, he crawled forward, towards the two guards, taking advantage of every bit of cover. Moving in similar fashion, Clint followed him closely. Slowly, they progressed to a point directly behind the guards, Wright and Slater, then stopped. They flattened down as Wright suddenly got up to walk over to look at the prisoners, before returning to sit down again by his partner.

Clint and Billy rose to their feet and silently moved up behind the two seated men. The aim of each of them was to stun his victim instantly by a blow to the head, Billy with his war club, and Clint with the long barrel of his Peacemaker. They struck simultaneously, hard and with precision. Both their targets slumped down, unconscious, without making a sound.

The two stunned men were quickly bound and gagged before they came to. Then Clint and Billy ran to the prisoners and freed them.

Clint spoke in a whisper to Dan and Josh. 'The two guards are taken care of,' he said. 'This is Billy. Father and three other men are waiting up the gully. Now we have to deal with the men in the tent. Are you two all right?'

They nodded their heads and Clint handed them the two six-guns taken from the guards. Then all four of them advanced on the tent. As they passed the fire, Clint accidentally knocked over a cooking pot, setting up a clatter from the loose spoons and forks inside it. With eyes fixed on the tent they halted for a moment, then moved on silently towards it. They had almost reached it when the flap was suddenly thrust aside and Perry came out with a six-gun in his hand. He fired at Clint, his bullet gouging the side of his victim's upper right arm. At the same time Clint fired back, narrowly missing his target. Firing at the same time as Clint, Dan shot Perry in the chest. Then, as Perry fell, Dan ran round him and into the tent, to encounter Morgan for what he hoped was the last time. But the tent was empty.

Dan shouted to the others that he was coming out. He left the tent and told them that Morgan was not there. Then they heard Jacob Kennedy calling from the other side of the fire. Dan told him and the three hands with him to join them. He pulled the dead body of Perry inside the tent, then spoke to them.

'Morgan's left camp for some reason,' he said. 'He could be coming back any time. We need to set a trap for him. But first let's take a look at that arm, Clint.'

The gouge was fairly deep, but the bullet was not lodged in the arm. Quickly, they padded the wound to stop the bleeding, then bandaged it. Then Dan asked Mailer and Sully to drag the two prisoners well up the gully, out of sight of the fire. Clint was to stay there with them to guard the prisoners. Jacob Kennedy told Dan about Ruth's arrival at the Rocking K. Then he and Prentice took up the positions on the ground previously occupied by Dan and Josh, who sat down where the two guards had stationed themselves. Billy was sent to hide near the entrance to the gully, to give advance warning of Morgan's approach.

'I can see you're limping, Josh,' said Dan. 'What's the trouble?'

'It's my darned hip,' said Josh. 'Started hurting when they tied us up in the gully here. Seems to be getting worse. Just old age, I guess. But it sure ain't going to affect my shooting.'

'You need to rest up a while when we get back to the ranch,' said Dan. 'Meanwhile, let's hope that Morgan rides into this trap we've set for him.'

They settled down to wait, but when dawn came with no sign of Morgan, it was decided that apart from Dan and Billy, they would all, after Perry had been buried, return to the ranch, taking with them Slater and Wright, both conscious but suffering from sore heads. Dan and Billy took up a position where they could hide and watch the gully for any sign of Morgan's arrival.

At the ranch house the women, waiting anxiously for their return, saw the approaching group of riders, and ran out of the house. Ruth's heart sank as she failed to see Dan. Then Jacob Kennedy told her that Dan had been found unharmed, but had stayed behind for a short while with Billy, in case Morgan showed up. Clint made arrangements for the two prisoners to be tied up and held in the barn, under constant guard. Then the family members and Josh all went into the house, while a hand was sent to Trasco to ask the doctor to come out and tend to Clint's wound, and also to advise on the pain in Josh's hip, which had worsened considerably during the ride to the ranch. When the doctor turned up he examined Clint's wounded arm, then cleaned the wound and bandaged it. He also provided a sling to be used for the next week or so. He told Clint that he must rest the arm to give it a chance to heal. Then he turned his attention to Josh. After an examination, he told his patient it was a clear case of a hip joint showing its age and protesting against activities which should be undertaken only by a younger man. He advised Josh to rest up for a spell before even thinking of climbing into the saddle again. After a quick check of the two prisoners he departed.

Two hours later, watching out for Dan and Billy, Ruth saw them approaching. She ran out to meet them, and she and Dan embraced, then went inside to join Jacob and Martha Kennedy. Dan told them that Morgan had not showed up. Martha said that Josh and Clint were both resting upstairs, under doctor's orders.

'I've got to say,' said Dan, 'I was mighty disappointed when I went inside that tent and found that Morgan wasn't there. He must have rode off somewhere before we turned up. I just can't think where. We can't let him get away. I'll ride around and see if anybody has spotted him.'

'Clint and Josh are laid up,' said the rancher, 'but we can get the hands to help you with that.'

'All right,' said Dan. 'I'll get something to eat, then we can make a start.'

Jacob Kennedy went out to speak to the hands, while Dan took a meal, during which he discussed the situation with Ruth. She told him that she would stay on at the Rocking K for the time being, in the hope that Morgan would soon be caught. Dan was just finishing his meal when the rancher came in with Billy Lightfoot.

'Billy here's got something to say to you, Dan,' said Jacob Kennedy.

'I was thinking,' sad Billy, 'that seeing as Mr Brennan is laid up, I could help you track Morgan down. I have followed the tracks of his horse before. I could pick them up at the gully.'

'You sure about this, Billy?' asked Dan. 'I reckon Morgan is alone just now, but he's a mighty dangerous man. You might get hurt, or even killed.'

'I am sure,' said Billy. 'Morgan is a bad man. I can see that he must be captured before he makes more trouble for your family.'

'Thanks Billy,' said Dan. 'With your help I reckon we have a good chance of catching up with Morgan. We'd best get on his trail while his tracks are still fresh. But first, Father, there's something I'd like you to do. If I write out a telegraph message to Ranger Captain Armstrong at Fort Worth, will you have it sent as soon as possible? I'm asking him to have the two prisoners collected from here. And to let the US marshal at Fort Smith know about Wilson at Comanche Wells, and about Truman, the crooked deputy US marshal in the Indian Territory. And I'll tell him that Billy and I are going after Morgan.'

'I'll see to that,' said the rancher, and Dan set about writing the message.

Fifty minutes later, after he had gone upstairs to

see Josh and Clint, he and Billy left, heading for the gully where Dan and his partner had been held prisoner.

THIRTEEN

Some time before the rescue party from the Rocking K had arrived at the gully, Morgan had ridden off towards the line shack, with the intention of ensuring that no surprise was being planned for him and his men when they took Dan and Josh there in the morning. He approached the shack with caution in the darkness and soon discovered that there was nobody there, and no sign of anyone having been there recently. He left the shack and headed back towards the hideout. He was drawing near to it when he stopped as he heard a short burst of gunfire ahead of him. He rode on a little, then dismounted, dropped the reins, and ran to a point from which he could look down into the gully. On the way, he passed by a group of eight picketed horses. Then, looking down into the gully, he could see men moving around near the fire. He decided that he must leave the scene immediately and move to a safe hiding-place. But the probable loss of the last two members of his gang fuelled his determination to wreak his vengeance on Dan and Josh in the near future.

He decided to ride to the border town of El Paso, picking up some provisions on the way. In El Paso there was a distant relative of his called Nolan, who had been a member of the Morgan gang for a while, until he had, with the proceeds of his criminal activities in the gang, taken over a saloon in El Paso. There, his profits were boosted by the crooked gambling activities of him and his employees. Morgan was sure that Nolan would shelter him temporarily, while he considered his next move.

The following morning, feeling the need for food, he stopped as he spotted the buildings of a homestead ahead of him. As he watched, a man and a woman came out of the house, climbed on to a buckboard, and drove off towards the north. Morgan waited till they were out of sight. Then he rode up to the house, checked that there was no one in or around it, and helped himself to sufficient food to take him to El Paso. When he eventually arrived there, he waited outside town until darkness had fallen. Then, from the rear, he approached the Rio Grande saloon, which he had visited a couple of times in the past. He tied his horse, then knocked on a door which opened into Nolan's private quarters at the rear of the saloon. The knock was answered by Nolan himself, who had come in there from the saloon only a few minutes earlier. He recognized

Morgan instantly and invited him inside. He led him to a small living room and they both sat down.

'I've been wondering where you were,' said Nolan, a stocky, well-dressed man in his middle forties. 'I heard about you losing most of your men. Are Kennedy and his partner still after you?'

Fuming, Morgan told him of the recent developments in the pursuit of him and his men by Dan and Josh. He said that he was aiming to kill them both as soon as the opportunity arose. But until things quietened down a little he would like to stay with Nolan at the saloon.

'Sure,' said Nolan. 'The rate is the same as last time. You can stay in my quarters here. There's a small room with a bed you can have. And you can eat in here with me. Where are Kennedy and Brennan now, d'you think? You don't reckon they've followed you here, do you?'

'Can't see how,' said Morgan. 'The way I came, even an Indian would have a hard time keeping on my trail. I reckon Kennedy and his partner have given up the chase for now.'

'I've just had an idea,' said Nolan. 'The Kelly gang moved down here from Kansas not long ago. I happen to know them pretty well. Kelly had two men with him, Yardley and Ryan. They took over an old abandoned cabin in a small canyon north of here. This is where they planned to operate from. I gave Kelly some information about a big gold shipment due to leave El Paso by express wagon three days from today. I overheard two men talking about it in the saloon. Kelly decided to hold up the wagon somewhere east of El Paso and steal the shipment.

'But just a week ago Kelly was shot dead here in El Paso when he paid a short visit to a store. As he went in he was recognized by a US marshal from Kansas who was on a brief visit to El Paso. As Kelly came out of the store, he was challenged by the marshal and a Ranger captain who was with him. Kelly went for his gun, but he had no chance. He was killed on the spot. And the Rangers had no idea where the rest of the gang might be.'

'What's all this leading up to?' asked Morgan.

'Well,' said Nolan. 'Kelly was the one who planned all their operations. It's something he had a talent for. The other two were pretty good at doing what they were told to do, but not particularly well-equipped in the brain department. So what they need is a new leader. As for yourself, although you ain't come off too good against Kennedy and Brennan, nobody can deny that before they turned up you carried out a long string of mighty successful operations. Seems to me you could maybe take Kelly's place. Apart from anything else, you're sure going to need some help if you're going after Kennedy and his partner. And another thing. I've seen Yardley since Kelly was killed. He visited me here after dark. He told me that he and Ryan don't feel like going ahead with the robbery without Kelly. They know your reputation, and I reckon they'd be glad to have you in charge if you agreed to help with the operation. What do you think?'

'I've missed out on two chances of getting a big ransom payment from Jacob Kennedy,' said Morgan, 'and I guess it's time I started making money again. How do I get in touch with Yardley and Ryan?'

'I'll take you there to see them right now,' said Nolan. 'I know where they are.'

They took a quick meal, then Nolan went for his horse and they rode out of town. They had ridden over an hour, under a clear sky, when Nolan stopped short of the entrance to a small canyon.

'Here's where we take good care not to be shot down,' he said, and shouted out his name a number of times, after which a reply indicated that it was safe for them to proceed. They rode up to the canyon entrance where Yardley was standing with a six-gun in his hand. He lit a match and took a close look at Morgan.

'Who's the stranger?' he asked.

'He's an old friend of mine,' Nolan replied. 'In the same line of business as you. He has a proposition for you and your partner.'

Yardley led the way to the cabin which was lit inside. Ryan was standing outside the door as they came up and the four men all went into the cabin.

Nolan introduced Morgan to the others, explaining briefly how he came to be a leader without a gang. Then Morgan took over.

'I had a run of bad luck lately,' he said, 'but for a

144

long time before that the Morgan gang did pretty well. And a new Morgan gang could do the same. For a start, we could take on this express wagon robbery that Nolan was telling me about. If you want to talk about me joining up with you, between yourselves and with Nolan here, I'll go outside for a spell. But understand that if I do join you, I'll be in charge. I wouldn't want there to be any doubt about that.'

Yardley walked to the door and opened it. 'We'll call you back in a few minutes,' he said, and Morgan walked out. Seven minutes later he was called back in and was told that Yardley and Ryan a were willing to accept him as leader of the gang.

Nolan left soon after, and Morgan and the others discussed the forthcoming operation. Morgan was told that Kelly had already chosen the point on the trail where the hold-up would take place. It was where the trail passed through a narrow gap between two low ridges, on the tops of which the gang could hide and fire down on the guards in the wagon.

'We'll go and take a look at that gap tomorrow,' said Morgan. 'Do we know anything about the express wagon that's going to carry the shipment?'

'It seems Nolan overheard quite a bit in the saloon,' said Yardley. 'Two wagon guards were talking, one of them a bit the worse for drink. From what he overheard, Nolan reckons the wagon will be an open one, of the sort he sees now and then in El Paso, with a driver on the driver's seat and two armed guards sitting inside.'

'We should be able to handle them,' said Morgan. 'Nolan tells me you're both pretty good with a six-gun and a rifle. But tomorrow, after dark, I'm going to see Nolan in town. We need another hideout to go to after the job's done. It would be too risky to come back here.'

The following morning they went to look at the gap through which the express wagon would be driven, and Morgan approved Kelly's choice of the spot where the hold-up should take place. They decided that they would leave the hideout during the night before the day of the robbery. Not being sure of the time of arrival of the wagon, they would take up their positions at daybreak, leaving their horses hidden on the far side of the ridge.

They returned to the hideout, and after dark Morgan rode into El Paso to see Nolan.

When Dan and Billy Lightfoot arrived back at the gully from the Rocking K to start their search for Morgan, there was just enough time before dark for Billy to find the tracks made by Morgan and his mount when they returned to the gully from the line shack. They stayed in the gully overnight, and took up the chase at daybreak. The tracks they were following led in a roughly westerly direction. Dan marvelled at the uncanny ability of Billy to see tracks which were completely invisible to himself. They kept up a steady pace, with Billy ranging a little way ahead of Dan, and in due course they arrived at the homestead which Morgan had raided for food. They told the homesteader who his unwelcome visitor had been, and said that he and his wife were probably fortunate to have been away at the time.

They continued steadily on their way, with stops for meals and rests, and Dan began to suspect that Morgan was heading for El Paso. This was confirmed when they came within sight of the border town and joined a wide trail leading into town from the north. The traffic along this trail had completely obliterated the tracks of Morgan's mount.

'It looks like Morgan may be hiding out in town, Billy,' said Dan. 'Or maybe he was just passing through. Let's go on into town and see the Ranger captain there.'

They found Captain Langford in his office, alone. Dan introduced himself and Billy. The captain, a brisk alert man, with many years experience of enforcing the law behind him, regarded the two with considerable interest.

'We've all heard, of course, of the way you and Brennan have been dealing with the Morgan gang,' he said, 'and we know he's been losing men fast. Are you still after him? And where is Brennan?'

Dan brought Langford up to date with the situation, and told him how they had followed Morgan from the gully to within sight of El Paso.

'He could be hiding out somewhere in town,' said Langford, 'or maybe he's crossed over into Mexico.'

'Or maybe,' said Dan, 'he's gone into hiding somewhere outside of town, this side of the border. Now Josh is a pretty good tracker, but Billy here is the best I've ever seen. What we'll do is circle round El Paso on this side of the Mexican border, and see if Billy can spot the tracks of Morgan's horse. If we turn up anything interesting, we'll let you know.'

'All right,' said the captain. 'Meanwhile, I have a Wanted poster on Morgan. I'll have it shown around town.'

Dan and Billy took a meal, then started on their search. They began it south-east of El Paso, on the bank of the Rio Grande, then started circling the town in an anticlockwise direction. They had reached a position north of El Paso, and well away from any of the main trails leading into town, when Billy stopped. He dismounted and knelt down for a closer examination of the ground. Then, bending down, he walked twenty paces to the north. He stopped, and motioned to Dan to ride up to him.

'These are the tracks of Morgan's horse,' he said. 'They were made maybe two days ago. But now he is riding with somebody else.'

'We'll follow the tracks,' said Dan. 'But you wait here, Billy, while I ride back and tell Captain Langford about this. I'll be back soon.'

On hearing the news Langford asked Dan to let him know if he caught up with Morgan and needed help. Dan said he would do this, then he rode back to Billy, who told him that a little way to the west he had found the tracks, leading back towards El Paso, of the rider who had been accompanying Morgan.

'I'm wondering who that could have been,' said Dan. 'But for now, we'll keep on following Morgan.'

They followed the tracks until, just as the sun was dipping below the horizon, they saw, in the distance, the entrance to a small canyon. The tracks they were following were heading straight in that direction.

'Morgan could be in that canyon,' said Dan. 'We'll wait here for an hour, then go and take a look at it.'

When they drew near to the canyon they stopped, then Billy went ahead on foot. He returned half an hour later to report that there was nobody inside, but there were signs in and around a cabin that more than one person had been there quite recently. He would be able to get more information at daybreak.

'Right,' said Dan. 'We'll ride on into the canyon, and in case anybody comes back in the night, we'll pick a place away from the cabin where we won't be seen.'

There was no sign of riders returning to the canyon before daybreak, when Billy had a good look round, before reporting back to Dan.

'Morgan was here,' he said, 'with two other men. Yesterday, before we turned up, they rode off to the east.'

'We'll follow them,' said Dan, and this they did until they found themselves approaching a gap in a low ridge ahead of them. As they drew closer they could see, just inside the gap, a stationary wagon, to which a team of four horses was harnessed. There was no sign of anyone accompanying the wagon.

'That looks like an express wagon,' said Dan. 'Let's go see what's happened there.'

Cautiously, they rode up to the wagon, holding their pistols. Shocked, they looked inside. Three men were lying on the floor of the wagon. All were motionless. An empty strongbox, which had been forced open, lay close to them. Dan dismounted, climbed into the wagon, and took a look at the three men. Two of them, wearing gunbelts, looked to be in their forties. The third was older.

'They've all been shot,' said Dan to Billy. 'Two of them, the guards, I reckon, are dead. The older man is shot bad, but he's still alive. I guess he was the driver. While I tend him, you have a look round for tracks, Billy.'

As Dan bent down to take a closer look at the driver, who had been shot twice in the chest, the wounded man's eyes opened, and he looked up at Dan, then at the two guards.

'Are they dead?' he asked in a voice which was barely audible.

Dan nodded his head. 'You're in pretty bad shape yourself,' he said. 'Where is the nearest doctor?'

'That would be El Paso,' said the driver, 'but I ain't sure I'd make it there. We were shot by three expert riflemen firing from the ridge. Didn't stand a chance. They came down to the wagon and checked us over. I played dead. But I sneaked a look at them when they were working on the strongbox.'

Haltingly, he went on to describe the three men as best he could. Then he sank back, exhausted.

'You rest now,' said Dan, noting that one of the men described could well have been Morgan. I'll do my best to stop the bleeding, then I'll take you to El Paso.'

Just as he was ready to leave, Billy rode up to report that after the robbery Morgan and the two men with him had laid a false trail to the north-east, but had then doubled back towards El Paso, riding parallel to the trail followed by the express wagon, and about 200 yards from it.

'You follow the tracks, Billy,' said Dan. 'I'll take the guards and the driver into El Paso. I reckon the driver might pull through if we get him there in time.'

Driving the wagon towards El Paso, Dan could see Billy on his right, following the tracks. As he came in sight of town, he saw that Billy was veering to the right. He lost sight of him as the wagon reached the buildings on the outskirts of town. He stopped outside the office of Ranger Captain Langford, who was just leaving the building. Langford walked up to the wagon, and looked inside.

'The guards are dead,' said Dan. 'The driver needs a doctor. He's hit pretty bad.'

The captain called out two Rangers who were in his office. He told them to take the driver to the doctor's house a little way along the street, then to get the undertaker to collect the two bodies. Then he and Dan went into his office, where Dan told him about their pursuit of Morgan and the two men he had joined up with; and of their discovery of the express wagon. He repeated the driver's sketchy description of the two men with Morgan, and told Langford that all three of them had headed back towards El Paso.

'Billy is following their tracks right now,' he went on. 'I'm hoping he'll be able to tell us whether they came into town.'

'I think I know who the two men with Morgan might be,' said the captain. 'A gang leader called Kelly was shot dead here last week, but his two men, Yardley and Ryan, weren't with him at the time. Morgan could have joined up with them.'

As he finished speaking, Billy came into the office. He told them that the tracks he had been following had partly circled town, and had then led up to the rear of the saloon and to what looked like a small stable belonging to it. He had watched from cover for a short while, and had seen two men leave the saloon through the rear door and walk the few yards to a cabin standing near to the rear wall of the saloon. They had gone inside, and had not come out again while he was watching.

'I've had my suspicions about Nolan, the saloon owner,' said Langford, 'and it don't surprise me to hear that he might be sheltering outlaws. They're probably staying out of sight in his private quarters and the cabin outside. We'll mount a surprise raid. I have four Rangers in town just now. With you and me, Dan, that should be enough.'

'Maybe I could help?' said Billy.

'Thanks for the offer, Billy,' said the captain. 'You've done a real good job tracking Morgan and the others, but I reckon you can leave the rest to the Rangers.'

As he finished speaking, a Ranger came in to report that the doctor had taken two bullets out of the driver, who was still alive and conscious. The captain told him to find copies of the Wanted posters showing pictures of Yardley and Ryan, and to ask the driver if these were two of the men who had robbed the express wagon. Ten minutes later the Ranger came back to confirm that Langford's suspicion was correct.

Another Ranger, having seen posters describing Morgan and the others, had been told earlier by the captain to go into the saloon on the pretext of buying a drink at the bar. He returned to say that there was no sign of the three inside the saloon. He said that Nolan himself was sitting in a game of poker, and looked like he might be there for a while.

'Right,' said Langford to Dan and the four Rangers who had assembled. 'We'll go now. First, we'll arrest Nolan in the saloon. Two of you Rangers will guard him with a shotgun, and keep order in the saloon. Then I'll go with one Ranger to the cabin, while Dan here, with the other Ranger, searches Nolan's private quarters. Let's go.'

It was an hour before nightfall. As they entered the noisy saloon a hush descended as the six lawmen walked over to the poker-players.

'I'm arresting you, Nolan,' said the captain. 'I'll explain why shortly. Just stay where you are for now.'

Leaving the two Rangers covering Nolan with a shotgun, Dan and his partner went through into Nolan's private quarters, while the captain and the Ranger with him left the saloon and ran round to the rear. Silently, they moved up to the cabin, keeping out of sight of the windows. They stood outside the door, holding their pistols. Cautiously, the captain tried to open it, but it was fastened inside. Immediately he motioned to his companion, a tall, muscular man, to throw his weight against it. It burst open, and the two lawmen ran inside. Yardley and Ryan, each of them resting on a bunk in the comfortably furnished cabin, were completely surprised. They had no time to reach for their weapons. Langford ordered them to lie face down on the floor.

'Shoot them if they move,' he told the Ranger, then ran out to see how Dan and his companion were faring.

When Dan and his partner entered Nolan's quarters, there was no one immediately in sight. Dan unlocked the rear door, then they looked in the rooms. All were empty except the last one they came to. Standing outside the closed door, they heard a brief murmur of voices inside. One was deep and gruff,

154

the other the high-pitched voice of a woman. Dan and his partner drew their six-guns. Dan tried the door, but it was fastened on the inside. He threw his whole weight at it, and the flimsy catch broke at the first attempt. Quickly recovering his balance, Dan ran into the room.

Lying on a bed at the far side of the room was Morgan. By his side was Lolita, the prettiest and most popular of Nolan's saloon girls. Morgan's reaction was immediate. He sat up, grabbing his six-gun from the bedside table with his right hand. At the same time, Lolita sat up and screamed as Morgan encircled her neck with his left arm. He held the pistol to her head, with the hammer cocked.

'Damn you, Kennedy!' he said. 'You and the man behind you, drop your guns on the floor, or this woman dies.'

Dan hesitated. He was sure that the outlaw meant what he said. Then the impasse was broken by Lolita. Unnerved by the pressure of the pistol against her head, she suddenly jerked up her left arm and knocked the end of the barrel upwards. The gun went off, the bullet embedding itself in the ceiling. Just for an instant, there was enough separation between the heads of Morgan and Lolita for Dan to risk a shot. He sent a bullet into the centre of the outlaw's forehead, just before Langford arrived to tell him that Yardley and Ryan had been captured.

Dan walked over to the bed and helped Lolita out. She was badly shocked, and he took her out of the room, then went for two of the other saloon girls to come in and comfort her. Nolan and the two outlaws were taken to the cells, and a search revealed, inside Nolan's safe, the proceeds of the express wagon robbery.

Before the telegraph office closed Dan sent a message to the Rocking K, telling them that Morgan was dead, and that after the trial of three of his accomplices Dan and Billy would be returning to the Rocking K.

The trial took place three days later. Yardley and Ryan were sentenced to death by hanging, the sentence to be carried out the following day. Nolan was given a long custodial sentence in the state penitentiary. Before Dan and Billy left for the Rocking K, Captain Langford told Dan that Truman, the corrupt deputy US marshal in the Indian Territory, and Wilson, at Comanche Wells, had both been arrested, and sufficient evidence had been unearthed to justify long spells in prison for both. He had also heard from Fort Worth that Wright and Slater, who had been taken there from the Rocking K, had both been tried and sentenced, Wright to death by hanging, Slater to a long prison sentence.

Then, impressed by Billy's tracking abilities, the captain offered him a job with the Texas Rangers. But Billy declined, saying that he was well settled on the Rocking K, and that he liked the work there.

'All right,' said Langford, 'but let me know if you ever change your mind.'

When Dan and Billy reached the Rocking K they found Clint fully recovered, and Josh ready to leave for Amarillo by stagecoach the following day. Ruth, greatly relieved that the long hunt had finally come to an end, was anxious to get back to her father. She and Dan left for Tremona by stagecoach the following morning, after taking their leave of Josh and thanking him for his help. On the way, they had a long talk about their plans for a future life together.

On reaching their destination, Dan first checked that no news had yet been received about the whereabouts of Johnny's aunt and uncle in California. Then he and Ruth sat down in the living room with Ruth's father. Dan told him that he and Ruth had talked over their future. He would leave the Texas Rangers and they would be married as soon as it could be arranged. Then, with money he had saved he would start running a small horse ranch as near to Tremona as possible. He had always been interested in horses, and figured on setting up as a breeder of quarter horses, much in demand by Texas cattle ranchers for cattle-handling operations.

'And then there's Johnny to think of,' he went on. 'Even if we find out where his folks are in California, we're not sure he really wants to go and live with them. We have the feeling he didn't get on too well with his uncle. Ruth and I are both fond of the boy, and we had the idea of adopting him and taking him with us to the ranch. You know how he likes working with horses.'

'I have an idea he'll jump at the chance,' said the liveryman. 'I'd sure miss him, but I know a man in town who'd help me out in the stable. Let's see what Johnny thinks of the idea.'

When Johnny came in a little later from the stable, and Ruth and Dan told him of their plans, and offered to take him with them as their adopted son, there was no need to ask him if their offer was welcome. The look of joy on his face gave them their answer.

A little later, Dan went upstairs to his room, and came down with the remaining Wanted posters, the ones for Morgan, Perry and Wright.

'No more need for these,' he said to the others, as he carried them over to the stove where, one by one, he consigned them to the flames.

BRANCH	DATE
NO	4/1/